AN ANA...

The Cost of the Crown

THE NETHERLANDS . 1541–1544

Claudia Esh

ISBN 10-digit: 1-933753-05-6
ISBN 13-digit: 9-781933-753058

Text and cover design: Teresa Hochstetler
Cover art: Lisa Strubhar
Printed by: Carlisle Printing

Carlisle Press
WALNUT CREEK

2673 Twp. Rd. 421
Sugarcreek, OH 44681

Dedication

Dedicated to all the heroes of the true Christian faith that kept the truth alive through the years, and to the Christian young people of today who have dedicated themselves to God and to the service of Christ our King.

The lines are fallen unto me in pleasant places; yea, I have a goodly heritage. I will bless the LORD. Psalm 16:6–7

Our Heritage

Don't forget your heritage,
Ye Christians of today,
For many others fought and wept,
While traveling this Way;
They feared and loved, they lived and died,
For the Almighty's love,
They smoothed the paths we travel now,
Leading us above.

In the Roman days of old,
Apostles spread the news,
Of endless love for everyone,
Though they be Greek or Jews;
They rallied 'round the cross of Christ,
And did not shrink or fear,
They lit the torch we carry now,
Burning bright and clear.

Through 'Dark Ages' they marched on,
A remnant small and weak,
The 'Church' fought hard against the ones
Who sat at Jesus' feet;
They believed the love of Christ above,
And trusted in His plan;
The gates of hell did not prevail—
God kept them in His hand.

When Reformation fires burned,
And many saw the Light,
When turmoil raged in Europe's plains,
The wrong against the right,
Then hundreds followed Christ their King,
Through fire and the sword;
They, even in the face of death,
Would not deny the Lord.

The cross and banner of the Lamb
Has triumphed through the years.
The blessings we enjoy today
Were sown in blood and tears.
So don't forget your heritage,
Oh followers of the Way—
Many others died for treasures
That are ours today.

Claudia Esh, July 9, 2006

Introduction

Some of my earliest memories are sitting on the floor beside Daddy's chair as he read or told me stories of my Anabaptist forefathers. When I learned to read, one of the first books he showed me was the *Martyr's Mirror* and I started to read the stories for myself. I'm very thankful that my parents took the time to explain to me what our ancestors have suffered because of their unshakable faith in the Word of God.

Margriete and Grietje, their families, and most of the major characters are fictitious, but many of the related incidents are factual as taken from the *Martyr's Mirror* and other books. All of the Dutch Anabaptist martyrdoms that the girls witnessed or heard about did actually take place.

I pray that this story will help us remember that the treasures of our heritage were bought with the blood of martyrs, and inspire us to press on and keep the holy doctrines that they died for alive in us. May God help us to be a generation of young people that stand for truth in our day as firmly as our Anabaptist forefathers stood for truth in theirs.

Contents

Name and Place Pronunciation

Aeltgen—AYL-chun

Anneken—AHN-ney-kuhn

Claes—CLAYSS

Doei—DOOIH (Good-bye)

Dokkum—DOLH-cum

Doopsgezinde—DOHWPS-chay-sin-duh (Baptism-Minded)

Enkhiuzen—enk-HWEE-zun

Friesland—FREEZ-lund

Frueder—FROWD-dur

Goedemorgen—CHOO-duh-mow-juhn (Good morning)

Grietje—CHRAY-cha

Jan—YAHN

Levina—La-VEEN-ah

Maeyken—MAY-kun

Margriete—mahr-GRAYT

Soetgen—SOOEHT-chuhn

Van Aernem—vahn AYHR-nuhm

Van Rijn—vahn RAYN

Zuiderzee—ZWEE-dur-see

Chapter 1

Questions and Conflicts

It was a quiet evening in the small town of Dokkum, Friesland. The sun was departing in all its majestic splendor, painting the sky with waves of soft pinks and brilliant yellows. A few seagulls circled lazily overhead, and small patches of gay wildflowers swayed slightly in response to the gentle breeze.

The silent beauty of the evening gave little evidence to the turmoil that was raging in the Netherlands. The year was 1541, and the Reformation was sweeping like a tidal wave over Europe. Educated men were challenging the Catholic Church, and Rome's hold on the continent was beginning to crumble. Sparked in Germany, the Reformation fire rapidly spread into Switzerland, Austria, England, the Netherlands, Spain, and France. The diverse churches—Catholic, Lutheran, Calvinist, Anglican, Anabaptist—vied for the minds and hearts of the common people. Separate state churches held sway over the districts of Europe, forcing the people under their control to comply with their demands.

And then—suddenly—handfuls of men and women began to rise up to challenge the newly established Reformed and the ancient Roman Catholic churches and traditions. Daringly defying law and custom, the Anabaptists brought Europe down upon them in rage.

A young girl, seventeen years old, rounded the corner of a well-kept cottage with a pail of fresh milk in her hand. She stopped, awed by the streaks of color illuminating the western sky. Her golden hair was tucked neatly under a white cap, and her clear blue eyes looked deep in thought.

She gazed into the beauty of the heavens, her thoughts straying into a long-forbidden zone: the Anabaptists. How well she remembered the many conversations about these strange people! Opinions varied wildly in Dokkum; some were hateful, some mocking, but most were sympathetic. And just when she tried her best to forget it all, something or someone would bring it back like a flood. So it was today.

It was an innocent walk, something to fill the rare spare moments of her day, until she passed two women whispering on the street. The girl did not linger, but she was walking slowly. She caught a soft word, "Anabaptists," then the guarded whisper, "Do you suppose they could be right after all?"

The whispered inquiry perfectly summed up her guilty

questions. And now as she watched the sun slide toward the horizon, the question haunted her. *Do you suppose?... Do you suppose...they could be right after all?*

Just then, a soft childish voice drifted out into the twilight. "Margriete."

The girl turned. "Yes, Janneken?"

The child looked out of the doorway. "Margriete, where are you? We're ready to eat supper."

Pushing serious thoughts resolutely aside, Margriete walked into the house. The room was simply furnished, with a large fireplace to the left of the door. In front of the fire stood a long, narrow table, neatly set. The children drifted to their respective places and bowed their heads for grace.

Around the supper table, the family talked and laughed over the events of the day. "It is being whispered over the town," Margriete's father lowered his voice, "that Menno Simons is coming to our area. He won't stay long—for safety's sake—probably only for a few days. He'll hold a meeting or two, maybe baptize a few people, and flee before the magistrates ever hear of it."

Margriete gathered up courage. "Father, what do you think of the Anabaptists?"

Her father raised his eyebrows slightly. "Well, Daughter, we've had so many groups of people that try to break away from the Church. Most of them die away or are put down by the authorities. Are the Anabaptists any different from the rest? I don't believe that Menno's right. How could he be? I don't understand everything, but—"

Margriete's mother cleared her throat and glanced meaningfully at the wondering eyes of the younger children. Immediately the serious conversation ended and the chatter of the children took its place, but a tense undercurrent remained.

Margriete sat staring thoughtfully at her plate, mulling over Father's words. Suddenly she shook herself. *Father said the Anabaptists are not right,* she told herself forcefully. *Just trust him. Forget about the whole thing.* She managed to keep her mind on happier subjects for the rest of the evening, talking about anything other than the conflicting religions sweeping the continent.

But as soon as she nestled between her down comforter, the troublesome thoughts came flooding back. She recalled everything she had heard about the Anabaptists. *They seem to be at peace,* she thought, *but don't they have heretical beliefs? They don't baptize babies, or pray to the saints…and what would happen to Friesland if everyone refused to fight?… But could it be that they are right and we are wrong? How can I know?*

"Oh, God," she whispered softly from the depths of her heart, "show me what is right."

It was Margriete's first real, heartfelt prayer.

Chapter 2

Decision at
the Market

Early morning light streamed through the open window, bathing Margriete's face as she washed the breakfast dishes the next morning. No more had been mentioned about the conversation the evening before, and Margriete's questions still hung defiantly in midair, begging for an answer.

The usual early morning work finished, Margriete prepared to leave for the market. She picked up a basket of fresh butter and cheese and slipped on her shoes. At the door, she turned slightly and waved. "Good-bye," she called brightly to her mother, who was hanging fragrant bunches of herbs to dry beside the fire.

"Good-bye, Margriete," her mother returned. How she appreciated her eldest daughter's help with the household duties that went with a family of seven children!

"Good-bye," little Pieter echoed from his place on the floor. Margriete waved at the two-year-old on her way out the door. She walked slowly down the cobblestone street, carrying her basket. Birds trilled happily in the majestic trees along the street, greeting the morning. Drops of dew still lingered on the flowers and leaves. The sky was cloudless, promising a bright, warm day.

But Margriete scarcely noticed the beauty of the scenery around her. Troubling thoughts dogged her footsteps, and her mind was far away. She knew that Menno Simons had been a priest in the small village of Pingjum earlier in his life. *Why* she thought, *would someone leave the comfortable, respected, easy life of a priest to become a hated, hunted 'hedge preacher'? When we go to Mass, we don't learn anything about God. We aren't even supposed to own a Bible. Why not? What is wrong with God's Word?*

Margriete tried to stop thinking; often she scared herself with the doubting ideas that insisted on returning. Unsuccessfully she tried to concentrate on the songs of the birds and the daisies nodding in the breeze. She was glad when she arrived at the market and could turn her mind to other things.

At the market, Margriete busied herself with selling her wares. The market was choked with men, women, and children, some eagerly advertising their wares, some shrewdly bargaining for things they wanted. Margriete's fresh butter and cheese sold quickly, for she was well known in the market for her superior goods. By mid-morning, her small collection of products was gone.

By noon, Margriete was ready to leave. She walked out of the market, glad to be finished with her buying and selling and out of the teeming crowd for another week. But she had gone barely three yards when she heard a cry behind her. She turned; a dark-haired girl about her age was running down the street toward her.

"Margriete?"

"Grietje!"

"Margriete," Grietje began slowly after a pause, "I was looking for you. I need to talk to you."

Something about her manner puzzled Margriete. Grietje was always carefree and impulsive, usually laughing about something. Today, however, something was different; her cheerful smile looked a little forced somehow, and her usual lightheartedness seemed strained.

The girls walked in companionable silence for a time, then Grietje cleared her throat and nervously smoothed a black strand of hair under her cap. "Margriete..."

"Yes?"

Grietje absentmindedly twisted her fingers together. "What will you be doing late Saturday evening?"

"'Late Saturday evening? Not much, I guess. Why?" Curiosity sparked in her eyes.

"Well...would you like to go somewhere with me?"

"Where?"

Grietje looked away. "Well...to an Anabaptist meeting."

Margriete's eyebrows rose the way they always did when she was shocked. "Grietje! Why? Where?"

Grietje smiled faintly, a shadow of a smile, really. "I heard there's a meeting in the forest. It was being whispered around the market today. You may have heard that Menno Simons is in the area?"

She lowered her voice to a murmur. "I want to find out what makes them different. I need to, Margriete. If we're arrested—which we probably won't be—we'll just tell them we aren't Anabaptists. They'll let us go. Will you go with me? Please?"

Margriete was silent for a long time. And when she looked at her friend, indecision clouded her eyes. "Grietje, what would my parents say? I will have to ask them, and…are you sure it's right? You know we've been warned. And it is so dangerous. But somehow, I want to. I don't know—I just don't know." Then she added, "How do you know they would let us come?"

Grietje blushed. "I've been there before." Then reading the fear and concern in Margriete's eyes, she said lightly, "Don't worry about me, Margriete. I don't intend to become an Anabaptist. It's far too risky. But will it do any harm to go to their meetings? Many of the people in this area are sympathetic without actually joining them. We likely won't be discovered."

"But if we are—" Margriete smoothed her apron nervously.

"I won't force you if you don't want to go, of course. But something in their faces attracts me—they're happy—happier than I am, even though their homes, possessions, and even their lives are in danger! I want to know why."

Margriete stared unseeingly at a patch of grass along the cobbles. "I do too, Grietje. If my parents allow it, I will go."

Chapter 3

An Illegal Meeting

Margriete was rather quiet when she arrived home. Her thoughts had been in a turmoil after leaving Grietje with her promise. Several times she regretted her decision, and the next moment she would be very glad that she had consented to Grietje's suggestion. After all, maybe…just maybe, the answers to her questions lay hidden in this opportunity.

Though Margriete tried her best to act as though nothing was the matter, she could not conceal from her mother that something was weighing on her mind. She ate very little food, was even quieter than usual, and didn't laugh at all.

Later that evening, Margriete's mother pulled her aside.

"Margriete," she asked, concern lacing her words and coloring her face, "is there something wrong? Did something happen at the market?"

For a long moment Margriete said nothing, but she had decided beforehand to tell her mother the truth. Quietly she replied, "Grietje asked me to go with her to an…an Anabaptist meeting. On Saturday evening."

Mother gasped in surprise and dismay. "Margriete! What did you say? Surely you will not go to—to that, will you?"

For the first time, Margriete raised her eyes to her mother's face. "Mother dear, of course I will not go if you forbid me to. But, Mother, I need answers to my questions. This may be the way to find them…"

Glimpsing a movement out of the corner of her eye, Margriete looked up and noticed her father standing silently in the doorway. She quickly realized that he must have heard every word that had been said. Fearfully she searched his face, hoping to read his thoughts. Margriete had never seen her father look so torn.

For a few moments, no one spoke. Finally Margriete's father broke the uncomfortable silence.

"Margriete," he said firmly, his mouth tightening, "I, too, have had doubts about the Holy Roman Church. You are young, but not young enough to be entirely protected from being caught up in the crosscurrents of the times. I don't want you to be swept in the Anabaptists' direction."

He stopped, brooding over something. Margriete saw deep emotion in his eyes, as though remembering something heartbreaking in the distant past. But then he looked up and continued, "However, the decision is yours. If you wish to go to this meeting, you may go. But—do you realize the danger that may be involved?"

Margriete looked into her father's eyes. "Yes, Father. Don't worry; this doesn't mean I'll join them. I just want to know more about what they believe."

Just then Gertrude skipped into the room. "Mother, there you are! I could *not* find you!"

"I'm coming, Gertrude. We were just having a little talk." The cheerfulness in her voice sounded strained, but the tense moment passed, and Margriete forced a smile for the sake of her family.

"Here, Janneken, can you sweep the floor quickly? And, Gertrude, will you pick up the pieces of wool that fell around the loom, please?" Margriete willed herself to relax and turned her mind to other things.

That night Margriete's mother tossed restlessly in her bed, worrying about Margriete. Her oldest daughter was so thoughtful, much more serious than most girls her age. Was it her imagination, or had she been paying close attention to the scattered tidbits of information about the Anabaptists? Horror filled her heart as she thought of her gentle Margriete being deceived by the spreading movement.

Not until it was past midnight did she finally drift into a fitful sleep, and then her pillow was wet with tears.

• • • • •

On Saturday evening, the children went to bed early, for the family would go to Mass as usual the next day. Margriete tiptoed to her room, smoothed out her skirts, and combed her hair carefully, shivering with excitement and a tinge of fear. Was she making a mistake? Standing at the door of her room, she wavered. Perhaps she should not go. But it was too late to turn back now. Grietje was expecting her. She couldn't let her friend down.

Margriete's soft eyes sobered at the thought of her father. He had surprised her by giving his consent. If the citizens of the town were hostile toward the growing movement, he would never have allowed her to go. As it was, most of the villagers would not think of betraying their kind Anabaptist neighbors to the rich and disdainful authorities.

She stepped into the kitchen, where her parents sat beside the crackling fire. She knew how apprehensive they were about their daughter attending the meeting, yet she also realized that they, too, especially her father, were searching for answers. Margriete turned to them. "Good-bye, Father and Mother."

Her mother looked up from where she was bending over her knitting, and Margriete saw tears in her eyes. "Good-bye, Margriete. Be careful."

Her father, however, had more to say. He cleared his throat and leaned forward in his chair. "Margriete, I might not care too much about religion, but I love you. You're a little quieter and more serious than some girls, but you're very determined, I know." His voice softened a little. "You're beautiful, Daughter, and I'm proud of you.

"Do pay attention to my guidance and don't let yourself be deceived. I believe I owe it to you to let you find the answers to your questions, but don't be foolish. Do you understand me?"

"Yes, Father," she murmured, raising her eyes and dropping them again.

Silently Margriete opened the door and stepped into the warm summer night. Millions of stars twinkled above the shadowy, silent streets, and a full moon gave her enough light to see her way. Here and there a lighted window dropped its glow onto the cobblestones, but most of the homes were dark and quiet. The trees were silent silhouettes against the moonlit sky.

Margriete walked carefully toward Grietje's house. She strained her eyes to see if her friend was standing there.

"Margriete?"

"Grietje!"

"You're here!" Grietje breathed. "I was beginning to be afraid your parents had forbidden it or something. Come. I know the way." She turned and picked up a lantern, turned low so as not to burn bright and alert the neighbors.

Silently the two girls slipped across a patch of grass and entered a thick forest. Margriete trembled slightly as they walked into the shadowy tangle of bushes and trees. The usually friendly woods was transformed into something monstrous and unfamiliar when darkness fell.

"Don't fall," Grietje whispered. "Here, hold my hand. We'll come to a path before long, then it will be easier." She was right, for soon Margriete could make out a thin crack in the thick timber, and they came to an uneven trail, cutting a narrow swath through the undergrowth.

Presently they saw a soft glow leaking out from between the trees, and Margriete's quick ears caught the sound of a low, quiet hymn being lifted to the starry sky. When they had rounded a corner, they could see a group of people sitting in a tiny clearing, dimly illuminated by a few lanterns. Though Margriete strained to recognize the men and women, it was too dark to see well.

Quietly Grietje sat down, motioning Margriete to do the same. They both knew the tune of the song well, but the familiar words honoring the Netherlands had been replaced by a story of a man, evidently an Anabaptist. Margriete was intrigued by the story. The man's name was Michael Sattler, who had been killed for the faith a few years before. She would ask Grietje about him later.

After the song had died away into the night, a man stood up and began to read aloud from a small black book. Margriete studied him carefully. He was probably around forty years old, worn from hasty travel. Grietje touched her arm furtively. "That is Menno," she whispered into Margriete's ear. Margriete nodded slightly, concentrating on what the speaker was saying. He was still reading.

"…And what shall I more say? for the time would fail me to tell of Gideon, and of Barak, and of Samson, and of Jephthae; of David also, and Samuel, and of the prophets:

"Who through faith subdued kingdoms, wrought righteousness, obtained promises, stopped the mouths of lions,

"Quenched the violence of fire, escaped the edge of the sword, out of weakness were made strong, waxed valiant in fight, turned to flight the armies of the aliens.

"Women received their dead raised to life again: and others were tortured, not accepting deliverance; that they might obtain a better resurrection:

"And others had trial of cruel mockings and scourgings, yea, moreover of bonds and imprisonment:

"They were stoned, they were sawn asunder, were tempted, were slain with the sword: they wandered about in sheepskins and goatskins; being destitute, afflicted, tormented;

"(Of whom the world was not worthy:) they wandered in deserts, and in mountains, and in dens and caves of the earth.

"…Remember the word that I said unto you, The servant is not greater than his lord. If they have persecuted me, they will also persecute you; if they have kept my saying, they will keep yours also.

"But all these things will they do unto you for my name's

sake, because they know not him that sent me.

"…Fear none of those things which thou shalt suffer: behold, the devil shall cast some of you into prison, that ye may be tried; and ye shall have tribulation…be thou faithful unto death, and I will give thee a crown of life…"

Some of Margriete's questions about these strange people were answered that night in the woods, but the experience also threw her soul into more of a turmoil than ever before.

• • • • •

Tears dripped slowly from the mother's eyes as she stared at the closed door through which her daughter had disappeared. She moaned softly.

"Maybe it's for the best," her husband comforted her, staring unseeingly at the fire. "Maybe Margriete's curiosity will be satisfied now, and she will forget all about these people. Margriete has always thought deeply about all she sees, and that incident in Delft three years ago unsettled her, I could tell."

His wife wiped her eyes. "In Delft? Did she know about that?"

"We didn't tell her, of course, but news has a way of traveling."

Her brows creased a little. "I'd almost forgotten about it myself." '

Claes gripped the edges of his chair in horror at the recollection. "Well, it was nothing less than a massacre. Twenty-seven men and women, all beheaded or drowned in less than a month! The poor people fled England because of persecution, but it certainly wasn't better here." He shook his head. "Also, there was that woman who gave her baby away… Margriete was quieter than usual for a week after hearing of that."

The mother sighed and crunched the hem of her apron with her fist. "I wish the authorities wouldn't be so hard on them, even though the Catholics are right, anyway. Still, I hate to see my own daughter being deceived like that! Maybe we shouldn't let her be with Grietje as much. Grietje was the one who invited her to this meeting."

Claes reached over and patted his wife's hand. "Don't worry. Margriete probably won't go to another meeting after this."

Chapter 4

What Shall I Do?

The next day as Margriete prepared to go to Mass, she was troubled to find that she did not at all wish to go. The ritual worship that her mother had taught her children to attend had lost its appeal. It seemed dry and meaningless compared to the rich words that she had eagerly drunk in the evening before.

As she watched the priest go about his holy duties, words that the preacher had read haunted her. "For there is one God, and one mediator between God and men, the man Christ Jesus."

The satisfied feeling that she had once enjoyed in believing that the priest had forgiven her melted away, leaving her with her guilt and doubts. Could it be that the things she had been taught from her childhood were false? The foundations of Margriete's religion were being shaken to the core.

On Monday Margriete walked down the street to see Grietje. She had to have answers for the questions that were bothering her. The two girls had grown closer now since they were going through the same struggles and facing the same decisions.

Grietje was toiling in the garden, pulling weeds around the half-grown plants, here and there watering a droopy stalk. Margriete bent down to help her, and after a greeting, the two girls worked in silence for a few minutes. Finally Margriete broke the silence.

"Grietje, did you enjoy the meeting Saturday evening?"

Silence. Grietje twisted a loose strand of hair around her finger. Slowly she replied, "Yes, I did. And, Margriete, more and more I begin to feel that they are right and we are wrong." Hastily she added, "I know you probably don't agree, but I've seen them more than you and have been to two of their meetings."

Margriete said nothing for a while. She ran her fingers gently around a slim blade. "I may agree more than you think. But is it worth such a heavy price as many of the Anabaptists pay? It frightens me, Grietje, to think of living in fear, hunted and outcast. I—I don't believe I could do it." Tears gathered in Margriete's eyes. "I know that my father may not mind so much, but what about my mother? If I would join them, it would break her heart."

Grietje stared at an earthworm burrowing into the coarse dirt. "But, surely, the truth, the real truth, is worth anything, even…worth dying for."

Margriete lifted her clenched hands to her heart. "Oh, Grietje, I can't!"

Grietje sighed deeply, toying absentmindedly with the folds of her apron. "I'm not quite as persuaded as I sound, perhaps. Sometimes I am sure they are right, and the next minute I'm convinced that they are wrong. I don't know what to do!"

They had finished in the garden, and both girls stood up. Grietje smiled at Margriete. "Thank you for coming and helping. *Doei!*" (Good-bye!)

"Doei!"

Margriete walked home slowly and prepared the noon meal. *I wonder...I wonder. Oh, God, how can I know what is right?* She wondered why God did not show her more clearly... *But of course! He did, in His Word! Oh, how I wish I had a Bible in my native language, or even a New Testament. Then I could see for myself. But it's a forbidden book. Maybe—*

"Margriete!" Janneken's insistent voice interrupted her thoughts. "You've been just standing there swishing that dish in the water for the last five minutes. Wherever are your thoughts?"

With an effort, Margriete brought herself back to the present and smiled at her sister. "I was just thinking, Janneken. I'm sorry." But no matter how hard Margriete tried to throw it aside, the question haunted her. "Who shall I believe? What shall I do?"

• • • • •

Miles away from the obscure town of Dokkum, city authorities from various parts of Friesland were gathering in the thriving city of Leeuwarden. They were determined to find the best and most efficient way to crush the budding movement of Anabaptism once and for all.

The room was old and scarred, bearing witness to the years it had been in use. The small windows shut out most of the sun's light and all of its warmth, and the air was cold and judicial.

"Locking up or executing the common people who have thrown in their lot with them simply doesn't seem to work," a gray-haired man was saying in exasperation, slamming his fist against the table. "Why, they even sing and preach on their way to execution and that influences dozens. Anyway, they slip through our fingers like eels, and even though hundreds have been burned or drowned already, thousands more are joining them!"

"We must find some way to capture the leaders," growled a heavyset gentleman, his mouth forming a tight line. "That's sure to stop them, for the leaders are the ones who spread the heresy. Without shepherds, those silly sheep are sure to scatter and race back to the true fold."

"That may be somewhat true, sir, but I find that nearly every member of this accursed sect seems bent on spreading their teachings. What shall I do? The more I kill the more they spread," the younger ruler whined.

The first speaker ignored him completely. He straightened up in his chair. "And we all know who the most prominent leader is—Menno Simons!" A general murmur of assent ran around the group.

Encouraged, the man continued, "Up to now, we have been unable to catch him. The man may be hopelessly deceived, but he is smart enough to know not to stay in one place very long. We have to have information—on where he is, what he's doing—so we can be prepared." He cleared his throat.

"We must offer a reward that will get us results. What if we offered some of his followers which are now in prison their freedom if they only gave us the information we need so that we could bring about his arrest?

"Already anyone that turns in an Anabaptist gets one-third

of his property, and some people make a regular business out of it. It's fairly lucrative if a man is shrewd. But they won't look for Menno. He doesn't even have a decent bed to call his own. It is highly possible that it will work. When it does, we will only be setting free one person in exchange for Simons."

He looked expectantly around the table. Heads nodded and a few affirmative grunts were heard. Then the heavyset gentleman spoke up. "But do we have the authority? We would do well to draw up a letter to her Majesty, Queen Mary of the Netherlands, and ask her for permission to carry out our plan."

Accordingly, paper, pen, and ink were brought, and the letter was duly written:

> Most serene, right honorable, most mighty Queen, most gracious Lady, we offer ourselves as humbly as we can for Your Majesty's service. Most gracious Lady, the error of the cursed sect of the Anabaptists has for years very strongly prevailed in this land of Friesland, but now the sect would doubtless be and remain extirpated, were it not that a former priest, Menno Simons, has roved about once or twice a year in these parts and has misled many simple and innocent people. To seize and apprehend this man we have offered a large sum of money, but, until now, with no success. Therefore we have entertained the thought of offering and promising pardon and mercy to a few who have been misled if they would bring about the imprisonment of the said Menno Simons...

The nets were tightening in the Netherlands, but the hunted ex-priest continued rallying the fledgling Anabaptist church around the blood-stained banner of the Son of God.

Chapter 5

"His Word
Is Powerful…"

The first pink rays of dawn were stealing over the horizon, touching Friesland's windmills and cottages with a rosy light. Light clouds scattered before the awakening breezes, giving promise of another sunny day.

Margriete rolled over in her bed, and then got up. She walked over to the window and sighed. She was tired—tired of the haunting questions, tired of the restless nights, tired of the decisions she was constantly being forced to make.

How she wished that she was a little girl again…carefree and happy, skipping over the dewy grass, exuberant at the opening of another day! *How I wish I never would even have thought about going to that meeting,* Margriete thought. *Ever since, I can't even enjoy seeing the sunrise.*

She knew that someday, somehow, she would have to decide who was truly following God's Word. This tiring limbo could not continue forever. *Surely it's worth anything to have peace with God.*

Wearily Margriete dressed and went to the kitchen to help prepare breakfast for their hungry family. Her mother was already there. "Good morning, Margriete," she greeted her cheerfully. Margriete forced a smile and returned the greeting.

After breakfast, Margriete picked up a pail and started for the barn to milk the cow. She had done this job so many times that she could have almost done it in her sleep, and many a time she was glad for an escape to the barn to milk and think. But now she dreaded the job, for whenever she had a chance to be alone, the troublesome conflicts would come rushing back like a tidal wave.

"Hello, Margriete," a merry voice sang out.

Margriete jumped, startled. "Grietje! Hello. I didn't see you at first."

"Well, I came to the house first, and Janneken told me that you were out here," Grietje replied with a laugh. Margriete noticed immediately that something about her friend's manner seemed different. She could not put her finger on exactly what it was that made her notice.

The girls chatted together for some minutes, then Grietje fell silent, as if wanting to say something and not knowing exactly how. Finally she said, "Margriete?" and her voice was almost a whisper.

Margriete was curious at once. She stood up and turned to face her friend. "Yes?"

"Margriete, two days ago I gave my life to God, and I want to be baptized before long." Grietje's voice carried a note of shyness, and she lowered her eyes, almost as if she and Margriete had not grown up together, as if she hardly knew her.

Margriete gasped in a mixture of surprise and fear. "Grietje! Are you sure this is what you want to do? Don't you know… what it might cost?" Margriete shocked herself by bursting into tears. She had known that her friend had been battling with the same things she was, but she had not guessed that Grietje's decision would come so soon.

Both girls thought of the many reports they had heard of Anabaptists being burned…beheaded…buried alive… drowned…all over Friesland and the rest of the Netherlands and Europe, and silence reigned for a few seconds.

Grietje's face sobered and she stared unseeingly at the ground. "Yes, don't think that I overlooked that. I thought about it long and hard. However, if I would die, I will go to be with my Savior. And, Margriete, I've found that this kind of assurance is worth dying for." She searched her friend's tear-filled eyes. "Oh, Margriete, how I wish that you could find God's peace, too!"

Margriete dropped down again onto the milking stool and buried her face in her hands. For several minutes neither girl spoke. Then Margriete raised her head and looked searchingly at Grietje, and she knew that every fiber of her being longed to possess what she saw in Grietje's eyes. Oh, why did it have to come at so great a cost?

Grietje said softly, "I have to go now, Margriete, but I want you to have this." From deep in a pocket in her dress, she drew a small, leather-bound book and pressed it into Margriete's hand. Grietje added wistfully, "I almost didn't accept it, for you know I can't read, but I thought of you. How I wish I could read it!" Almost unaware of what she was doing, Margriete hid it in the folds of her apron.

"Good-bye, Margriete."

With a smile and a wave, Grietje was gone. After her friend had disappeared, Margriete drew out the little book and looked at it curiously. Why, it was a Bible! Well, not quite, only a New Testament, but in her own language! Wonderingly, cautiously, Margriete opened the little book. She had been told for as long as she could remember that only the well-educated priests could understand the Holy Writ, and that if a common person attempted to read it, he would be led astray.

"Come unto me, all ye that labour and are heavy laden, and I will give you rest. Take my yoke upon you, and learn of me; for I am meek and lowly in heart: and ye shall find rest unto your souls. For my yoke is easy, and my burden is light."

Margriete's heart reached out, searching, searching, for what? Wide-eyed, she hungrily read half of a chapter before the cow's impatient tail jerked her back to reality. Quickly she began milking, shoving the book far into her pocket.

Suddenly she realized that she was in the possession of a forbidden book, and there would be dire consequences were she ever to be caught with it. *I will never let anyone else see it—not even my own family,* Margriete thought firmly. *But… what could be wrong with reading God's own Word?*

The rest of the day Margriete watched the clock's hands inch past the hours, waiting for evening to come, when she could read her book in peace and secrecy. She was quiet through supper, rushed through the dishes, and rejoiced when her younger siblings went to bed.

After saying 'good night' to her parents, Margriete quietly tiptoed to her room with a candle, as usual. She shut the heavy door firmly and sat down on her bed. Carefully she pulled the small volume out of her pocket, then sat looking thoughtfully at the leather cover. How glad she was that her parents had insisted that she go to the parish school when she was young! Margriete had never seen any sense in the idea—the family, and all their neighbors had almost no reading material—but now she rejoiced that she had obeyed.

Absentmindedly Margriete fingered the thin cover, remembering when she had first heard of an Anabaptist being martyred. It had been two years before, when Margriete was only fifteen…

"Did you hear what happened in Delft?" the town gossip, a thin, angular woman, had whispered confidentially to another woman just outside the open window.

"No, what is it?" her companion asked, her brows creasing curiously.

"There was this woman named Anneken, who was arrested, charged with heresy. Her husband had recently died and she had a baby son with her in prison. Well, after a few months she was sentenced to be drowned. On the way to the canal, crowds lined the streets to see her go. They say she held up the child and said, 'I have a son who is three-quarters of a year old. Who will take him?' A poor baker, who already has six children of his own, volunteered to raise the baby, so Anneken handed him her son, with some coins tied up in a handkerchief. She was drowned in the canal and that was the end of the matter." The gossip laughed a thin, hardened cackle.

The two women had meandered away, and Margriete had slammed the window to the street in disgust.

The creaking of the branches in the breeze jerked Margriete roughly back to reality. Her gaze fell again on the forbidden New Testament. Slowly, cautiously, she opened it. The pages fell apart to the first chapter of the Gospel of John.

"In the beginning was the Word, and the Word was with God, and the Word was God. The same was in the beginning with God. All things were made by him, and without him was not anything made that was made..."

Margriete read long into the night. She never heard the clock over the fireplace in the kitchen chime the hours of 12:00...1:00...2:00. She was lost in the pages of the Holy Scriptures, drinking in the words of life. Many times she was shocked at some verses that she read, comforted by others, frightened by others.

At about 3:00 in the morning Margriete closed the little book, thoroughly shaken. All that she had been taught by her devout mother—all that she had ever learned and believed in—lay in ashes at her feet. *Why, if you interpret those words literally, all the doctrines that I have been taught from my childhood up are wrong!* she thought in disbelief.

Margriete sat on the side of her bed for a long time. She knew that the decision she had to make would decide what her life would be like. She could cling to the principles that she had been taught and live a quiet life in peace and safety, or she could forsake them and live a life of danger and peril.

But there was more that would be decided...her eternal destiny. The sheltered girl shrank desperately from what she would face if she chose to live only by what she had read this night. "'...Be thou faithful unto death, and I will give thee a crown of life,'" she whispered into her clenched fingers. "Oh, Lord, why must it be so hard? *Why* must the cost be so great?" She knew that her father, while he would not be pleased if she was rebaptized, wanted her to choose what she felt was right. But her mother, who had tried her best to raise her children as good children of the Holy Catholic Church, would be heartbroken if her eldest daughter became a 'heretic'. *Dare I? Can I bear the price?* Margriete deliberated in dread. *But surely, heaven is worth everything.* She was cold, then hot; softly she rose and threw open the shutters, then reseated herself on the bed.

For a long time not a sound disturbed the peacefulness of the night. The flickering candle had dripped down into a short stub in a hardened puddle of wax on the holder, but it still dimly illuminated Margriete sitting motionless by the window, fingers tightly clenched, struggling silently with her soul.

She thought about her sins—she had committed them, she knew. All the little lies—petty stealing, snappy words, rebellious thoughts—passed before her in a seemingly endless train. There was pride too—she had been proud of her family, proud of her nation, her abilities, even her attractiveness.

Finally Margriete slid off her perch on the bed and knelt on the wooden floor. Her white cap had fallen off her flowing hair, so she pulled it back on instinctively. Slowly she folded her hands and buried her head in the quilt. There, in the silvery light of the moon, she gave her life to the Almighty God, confessing her sins and asking Him to help her through the days ahead.

After a long time, Margriete rose from her knees to a new and dangerous life. Though she had made a decision that would cost her everything, Margriete slipped into her bed and slept with a peace that she had never known.

Chapter 6

The Melted Candle

awn was lighting the east in the morning when Margriete awoke. She rose and dressed with a new, quiet solemnity, for she knew full well the consequences of the path she had chosen. She realized that from now on, danger would haunt her footsteps, and that this decision could cost her her life. She knelt by her bed again and pleaded for God's grace to guide her through the day and through the days ahead. Her life was no longer safe and predictable, and sometimes Margriete shuddered when she thought of what the future might hold.

Margriete knew that she needed to tell her mother of her nighttime decision, but she dreaded the prospect. She loved her mother, and Margriete hated to hurt her. Quietly she made her way to the kitchen.

"*Goedemorgen* (good morning), Mother."

"Goedemorgen, Margriete." The mother smiled over her shoulder, on her way to Margriete's room with her daughter's shoes. Pushing open the door, the woman stopped suddenly and shook her head in puzzlement. She picked up the candle-holder, drowned in stiff white wax. Dropping the shoes on the bed, she took the holder, candle remains, and all in her hand and reentered the kitchen.

"Margriete," she said, not unkindly, "whatever were you doing last night? Why, you must have been up past midnight, by the looks of this candle. Couldn't you sleep, or what?"

Margriete looked away. "I was reading."

The mother set the candle down on the table. "Reading? We don't have anything to read. What did you borrow?"

Margriete drew a nervous breath. "Grietje gave me a New Testament, Mother."

"Margriete Emkens! A *what?*" Her hands flew to her throat.

Margriete forced herself to meet her mother's eyes. "A New Testament."

Her mother stood in shocked silence for a long minute. Tears began to pool in the corners of her eyes. "Daughter, you smuggled an unlawful book into our house and read it last night without my knowledge? I would never have guessed it of you! Bring it to me."

Pain etched over Margriete's face. Was it really necessary to break the terrible news? Maybe—but...

"Mother," Margriete began slowly, copying the way Grietje had broken the same news to her, "you don't understand. This morning I gave my life to God, and I want to be baptized before long."

The graying woman stared at her oldest daughter for several long, awkward seconds. Then, without saying a word, she almost collapsed into the nearest chair. She covered her face with her apron and began to cry, her tears soaking the snowy fabric. Margriete stood helplessly in the middle of the room, watching her. A deep ache gripped her heart as she watched her mother weep.

What have I done? she thought sorrowfully. But the new serenity that she had just begun to taste settled over her again, and she felt calmed, even though she hurt with her mother. And through this first painful crisis was the quiet assurance that she had done right.

For the rest of the day Margriete's mother was very quiet, only speaking to her oldest daughter out of necessity. *Tonight, when the little ones have gone to bed, she will tell me more about how she feels,* Margriete consoled herself. *At least I hope so.* She could not remember ever seeing her mother this disturbed and depressed.

Of course, it was natural for a mother to be heartbroken over her young daughter denying the principles that she had labored so hard to teach, but somehow Margriete's knowledge that she was the cause of her mother's sorrow tore the girl as she had not expected. The two had always been very close, but Margriete's decision abruptly ripped a painful and unanticipated gulf between them. *Oh, God,* Margriete thought, tears threatening to spill, *will it ever be fully healed again?*

Margriete's younger siblings caught a bit of the despondent mood and were unusually silent, and the day passed slowly by.

That evening, after the family had gathered around the well-worn table and thanks had been given for the food, Margriete's father had news. "It sounds as though the authorities are becoming more and more determined to stamp out the

Anabaptists," he said, fingering his spoon handle.

"Quite a few of the men at the mill were discussing it today. Four Anabaptists were arrested in Wormer. They've been brought as prisoners to Enkhiuzen, just across the Zuiderzee. Two of the men's first names are Pieter; that's all I know."

Mother gasped a little and glanced at Margriete. Margriete thought she knew what her mother was thinking—*What if that would be my daughter?*

"What will they do with them?" inquired ten-year-old Cornelius, always curious. He shoveled another bite of food into his mouth.

"I don't know, Son," was the thoughtful reply. The man looked at his son as though he was not really seeing him. "Release them, maybe, if they recant their beliefs. For their sakes, I hope they do. This tyranny from Spain is such a burden. What right does a church, no matter how correct it is, have to force its doctrines on others?"

Margriete's mother looked up quickly. "Oh, Claes!"

He lowered his voice and turned back to his plate. "Don't worry; I don't voice my opinions to anyone but you."

"Why are we talking about someone we don't know and something that doesn't affect us?" little Dirk asked impatiently, motioning for the bread. "I'm hungry!"

"You're always hungry, aren't you, little brother?" Margriete laughed, reaching over and tousling his sandy hair.

The rest of the meal passed in a strained quiet, mostly because the mother, usually talkative and cheerful, was eating her food in almost total silence. Margriete noticed her father cast several worried glances at his wife, and the younger children lost their chatter for once and were looking anxious and frightened. Never had they seen their mother so disturbed.

Margriete had known that her decision would hurt her mother deeply, yet she had not expected such obvious despair.

It troubled Margriete, and stealthily stole some of the sweetness of the peace she had recently gained. She knew that her father would undoubtedly be told this evening, and she wondered what his reaction would be. Surely he was being prepared for a shock by his wife's crushed behavior.

Slowly Margriete helped with the dishes. She was not nearly as ready for the evening to pass as she had been the evening before. Restlessly, she churned the butter and scrubbed out the blackened pots. Finally the younger children were tucked into their beds. Margriete fought back an urge to join them; she was tired and was dreading the discussion with her father more every second.

"'Whosoever therefore shall confess me before men, him will I confess also before my Father which is in heaven,'" Margriete quoted softly to herself as she entered the kitchen. Her parents were seated on chairs drawn up close to the fire.

Her father's forehead was creased in perplexity, and worry shadowed his face. Her mother's shoulders were bowed as if under a heavy burden; she did not meet her daughter's eyes. Silently, Margriete seated herself on a chair close to her mother, steeling herself for the confrontation to come.

After what seemed to Margriete an eternity, Mother broke the silence. She did not waste words, but went directly to the dreaded point. "Claes, Margriete told me this morning that she would like to be...be...rebaptized and join the Anabaptists." With that, she hid her face and burst into tears.

Margriete was watching her father closely, hoping he would not take the shocking news too hard. She saw his mouth tighten in concern and Margriete thought she read fear in his eyes.

"Margriete," he finally said slowly, as though feeling his way, "I hope you realize the cost of such a thing. I don't want my own daughter to be tangled up in that mess.

"Remember the Munsterites? They revolted against the authorities, seized the city of Munster, and, in short, most of them were starved, killed by diseases in the city, or put to death by the Catholic army. One of their leaders is even now in prison—he has been there for seven years—and has radically changed his beliefs."

Margriete's mother breathed a ragged sigh of relief. Perhaps rational reasoning could sway her daughter where pleading could not. But Margriete was saying calmly, "I know, Father, that the Munsterites were wrong in their teachings, and that they were cruelly put down. However, I believe most Anabaptists strongly disagree with the Munsterites. They are more closely following the Bible's teaching; they would never fight to save themselves."

Margriete saw her father's eyebrows lift, and he pursed his lips. "The Bible? How do you know what it says about such things?"

"I have one, Father." Margriete knew that what she would have to admit would disturb her father, and she was not wrong. His face darkened, and he moved as if to rise from his chair.

"A forbidden book, owned by my own daughter, here in my own house?" His voice had risen. "Margriete, I may be more lenient than most fathers when it comes to my children's beliefs, but I *am* a law-abiding citizen, even though I can't say I appreciate the laws. I cannot allow such things to go on under my roof."

"Father, please," Margriete pled, brushing a damp curl off her cheek. "No one will ever hear about it. I promise. At least…" she hesitated, "no one that is not trustworthy."

"I will think about it for a bit, Margriete, but I don't like it." His voice had quieted a little. "Anyway, you're in no real danger until you're baptized. Couldn't you just serve God however you please without being baptized? I love you. I don't want to see you fleeing for your life like a scared hare."

"I know," Margriete almost whispered. "I don't want it either. But I've chosen to follow God, and I must, no matter what the cost. I am commanded in His Word to be baptized, and I will obey Him." A long, strained pause followed. Margriete's gaze pulled toward the crackling flames.

"God doesn't promise us that we won't have persecution, but He promised, '…be thou faithful unto death, and I will give thee a crown of life.'"

Silence.

Chapter 7

The Fires
of Enkhiuzen

After the first despairing day, Margriete's mother, for the sake of her younger children, pretended that all was well, and relative peace settled over the household again. Only Margriete and her fourteen-year-old sister, Lijsken, could still see her sadness. "Why is Mother acting so strangely?" asked Lijsken two days later in perplexity. "She's just not herself. Do you think she could be getting ill?"

"No, Lijsken," Margriete replied slowly, shaking her head. "I will tell you why, but please promise me that you won't tell anyone outside our family."

Breathlessly, Lijsken promised. "Of course, Margriete."

"Well, the reason that Mother is so depressed is that I would like to be baptized and join the Anabaptists." Margriete wondered how many more times she would need to explain her decision to others.

Lijsken's eyes widened and she gasped, "Margriete! I cannot, I simply cannot, believe it! What will happen to you?"

Margriete managed a smile at her sister. "Remember, Lijsken, I haven't been baptized yet. I'm not in any immediate danger. After I have been baptized, I will be; however, most people in this area are disillusioned with the Catholic Church and rather sympathetic to the Anabaptists, you know. Don't worry about me."

· · · · ·

Three days later, Margriete's father arrived home with more news. "Remember those four Anabaptists that were arrested in Wormer? They've been sentenced now, to be burned at the stake."

The sudden and brutal sentence did not really shock Margriete; nevertheless she felt fear's icy fingers squeezing her heart. "When?"

"In two days. I will actually be in Enkhiuzen in two days. Of all men, they picked me to go there."

"Why, Claes?" Margriete could tell that her mother was not at all pleased.

"On business." His eyes twinkled at his wife in forced gaiety. They sobered again as he glanced at Margriete, and she knew that he was afraid for her, but Margriete's eyes did not falter. *O Lord, help me! This decision could cost my life...but I must obey You... I must.*

That evening, after dark, Margriete joined Grietje at the corner. Both girls were trembling visibly with excitement and fear. Tonight they would be baptized upon their confession of faith, a solemn vow, a covenant with God!

The trees were silhouetted against the moon, its silver sheen dimming the stars. The two girls crept hand in hand to a small, modest cottage on the outskirts of the town. A few flickering rays of candlelight escaped the heavy shades that were drawn over the window.

There were only a few people present, but they rejoiced. Two souls had been added to the church of God in Friesland! Despite the fierce persecution, the relentless threats, the cruel Spanish Inquisition, the work of God would go on in the Netherlands!

After a short sermon, Grietje and Margriete knelt and were baptized with a handful of water. Margriete rose soberly, knowing that she was rising to face serious danger because of the step she had taken. But somehow, at the same time, she felt a peace—a wonderful peace that she had never known before.

At the close of the quiet service, a slender woman named Verena approached the two girls with a friendly smile. Margriete and Grietje knew her by name, but not much more. Verena was unmarried and in her thirties—not especially beautiful, but radiant in her love for Christ. Her round face and rich accent betrayed her Swiss heritage.

"I know you two girls are busy at home," Verena began with a tinge of apology in her voice, "but I also know that both of you would like to study God's Word with others to help you grow in your Christian life. If you would like to come to my home sometime to do that, you are very welcome."

"Of course!" Grietje assented quickly, her eyes shining, and Margriete smiled her acceptance.

They walked home in silence. At the corner, where Grietje left Margriete, the two girls embraced in the darkness. "God be with you, Margriete."

"And with you, Grietje. Doei!"

When Margriete's father returned home from Enkhiuzen, he was shaken. Late that evening, when everyone except Margriete, Lijsken, and their parents had gone to bed, he told the story.

"There were four of them, as I told you, Dirk Krood, Pieter Trijnes, Claes Roders, and Pieter Jans, all burned alive. It was an awful sight, I tell you. There were soldiers all around, and there was a platform with four stakes on it. The men didn't seem to fear it at all. They were singing as they were being led to the platform. The words were:

'Veel lieuer kies ick ongemack,

Al met Gods kinderen te lyden,

Dan ick van Pharao ontfang sijn schat,

Om een cleyne tijt met hem te verbliden....'

('I'd rather choose the sorrow sore,

And suffer as a child of God

Than have from Pharaoh all his store,

To revel in for one brief while...')

"I forget the rest. They sang until they had no more breath in them. One of them wanted to speak to the crowd that was gathered to see it, but the soldiers wouldn't allow it. The people were very restless; it was plain to see that they did not like what was going on. It was amazing, those men. One of them couldn't have been more than thirty years old, and singing like that..."

Margriete could tell that her father had been touched. She desperately hoped the men that had been offered the day before would not have died in vain. "Lord, save my father. Lead him to the truth," she cried as she knelt beside her bed that evening.

Chapter 8

Haunting Memories

A sharp rap on the door startled Margriete as she stood scrubbing the breakfast dishes. Her mother went to the door. Within minutes she was at Margriete's side.

"Old Elizabet has had a bad cold for several days," she murmured. "That was her daughter, wanting me to come see what I can do. It's probably not serious."

Margriete nodded, smiling affectionately at her mother. She was known over Dokkum for her almost miraculous touch with herbs, and was often called on such missions as this. With a smile and good-bye, she was gone.

"Margriete?"

Margriete whirled around, her skirts brushing the smooth wall. "Father!"

"Margriete, come sit down. The children are playing, and you and I need to talk."

A stone settled in Margriete's stomach. Slowly she sat down opposite her father. She and her father had not had a long, deep conversation since she had made a decision to be rebaptized almost a week before. Would he try to convince her to give up her faith?

"Margriete, do you remember what happened three years ago in Delft?" He gazed past his daughter, lost in memory.

Margriete's brows creased, and she smoothed a flaxen curl under her cap. "Slightly. I didn't hear much about it at all."

"That was because your mother and I agreed that you were too young to bear it. That may well still be true, but I feel you need to know what could happen because of your rebaptism."

Silence fell—a heavy silence, made sad by a father's sigh. "I tried to forget that event, Daughter, but I simply couldn't. I had been a loyal Catholic, but it forever changed my views toward the Roman Church."

Margriete leaned forward. "Tell me."

He sighed again and drummed his fingers on the tabletop. "Well, it's like this. It all started in England, when a group of people there joined the Anabaptists. However, the persecution was so severe that they fled to the Netherlands, where they hoped to find refuge.

"Within a few months, the authorities in Delft had captured all twenty-seven of them while they were at a meeting. They were rushed through a fake trial and condemned. The men were beheaded and the women were drowned. It was terrible...terrible." He buried his face in his hands. "Delft was a grim city for weeks, and a great tide of sympathy turned toward the Anabaptists."

Margriete shook her head in numb shock. "You and Mother were actually in the city, weren't you?"

She saw his fingers trembling with emotion. "Yes, we went to visit an old friend and left you and the rest of the children at your aunt and uncle's house for several days. Your mother and I, unfortunately, happened to see several of the men being executed. We didn't stay. It was simply awful, Margriete. And now with the men of Enkhiuzen…"

Another long silence settled over the two of them as they thought of the massacre. Suddenly the father raised his head and looked deeply into his daughter's eyes. "Margriete, look at me. I want you to understand something. I may not be very faithful in going to Mass, but I am not a—a sympathizer toward the Anabaptists. I simply think they should be dealt with more tolerantly, not that they are right. And I am not overjoyed about you joining them."

Sadness clouded Margriete's deep blue eyes. "Yes, Father, I know."

His voice softened. "Margriete, you are growing into a beautiful young woman, and I love you very much. Think about what I have just told you. Will you throw away your life like that? Consider the cost, Daughter; this is not a decision to be made lightly.

"Dozens of men and women have died already, and the authorities are not likely to have mercy even on a girl. It hurts me to tell you this, but I really believe that you have made the wrong decision, not because of the beliefs, but because of the cost."

Margriete clasped her hands. Her glance flashed toward the window, then back to her father. "Father, I must follow the path of the teachings of Christ. My life would be a small price to pay for all that my Savior has given me."

He rose heavily and started for the door. His daughter was a decisive person, he knew, and it was obviously useless to attempt to change her mind now. With his hand on the latch, he turned and looked back. "Margriete, I pray with all my heart and soul that it never will come to that."

Chapter 9

Verena and the Letter

Early one cloudy afternoon, Margriete walked to Verena's home, her precious New Testament hidden securely in her pocket. How thankful she was for it! The fact that Grietje could not read was somewhat compensated by her parents, who were also Anabaptists and wholly supported their daughter's decision. Many times Margriete felt that without her tiny volume of Scripture, she could not have stood against the ever-tightening pressure.

"Young people, you do not know what may happen in your future," a man had told them soberly several weeks before.

"Hide God's Word in your heart, for then no man can take it from you!" The warning was hardly needed; Margriete and Grietje had been memorizing verses daily, almost feverishly, always preparing for the net of persecution being drawn steadily around them.

Rain began to fall as Margriete neared Verena's cottage. The room that she gratefully stepped into was small but clean and neat, and a fire was crackling merrily, making the shadows dance over the simple furniture.

"I wanted to study with you," began Verena when Grietje had arrived, "but there is something else, too." She stopped and took a deep breath, as if trying to decide where to begin. "I may as well tell you the whole story.

"Twelve years ago, there was a young woman in Flanders named Rachel Louvain. She was of the Doopsgezinde who are in Switzerland, was married, and had a three-year-old son. She was so active in persuading other women to join the cause that the authorities purposed to end the matter once and for all. She was captured, and quietly but quickly condemned.

"In just a few weeks, she was secretly drowned in prison. Her son was taken away from her a week prior to her execution, and, knowing what was to happen to her, Rachel smuggled several letters out of prison."

Verena's eyes mirrored anguish. "Rachel wrote a long letter to her son. To one of her trusted friends, a girl several years younger than herself, she wrote a heartbreaking note, begging her to keep the letter until the boy was older; and to try to know where he was living at all times. She desperately wanted her son, who would undoubtedly be given to a Catholic family to raise, to receive the letter.

"The girl was true to her promise, and knows where the

boy is. His surname was changed, but he knows that his foster family are not his parents. He believes that his parents drowned accidentally in a flood."

Margriete was mystified. What was Verena's story leading up to? And then Verena shocked both girls by bursting suddenly into tears. "Rachel was my dear friend, and I am that young girl," she admitted to her stunned listeners. From a hidden pocket in her dress, Verena pulled out several carefully folded and sealed sheets of paper. "Here is Rachel's letter to her son, now Jan van Aernem."

Margriete gasped. The blacksmith's adopted son! An image of Jan's brooding face and dark, menacing eyes rose before her. It was common knowledge in Dokkum that Jan hated the Anabaptists in Friesland with a vengeance. How would he react to a letter from his own mother, now dead for many years? Would he toss it aside, believing it to be a cruel joke?

"I suppose I will keep it for now, at least," Verena said, regret shading her words. "He will never receive it as his mother prayed for him to, at least for now. Pray for him, girls. I have kept Rachel's secret for fifteen years, but I had to tell someone. I—I—if anything would happen, I wanted someone to know."

Verena replaced the letter in her pocket with a sigh. The three women bent over Verena's Bible, always preparing for a time when the thick clouds of persecution hanging darkly over their heads might suddenly burst into blood and fire and tears.

That night, kneeling by her bed, Margriete added, "And, Lord, please do something in Jan's heart. Show him, somehow, the way to the light. Create some circumstances that show him his sin…"

How could she know how soon—and how unexpectedly— her prayer would be answered?

Chapter 10

A Traitor in Dokkum

Margriete, can't you reconsider?"

It was Margriete's aunt Esta. She loved Margriete dearly, and was distraught when she learned of Margriete's decision to leave the church of her birth. And on this lovely fall morning, when Margriete breezed cheerfully in with a basket of fresh grapes, Esta confronted her niece.

"Aunt Esta, I cannot," Margriete answered as gently as she could, resting her hand on the doorpost. How hard it was to have her own family beg her to deny her faith!

Her aunt adjusted the strings of her apron. "But, Margriete, you are young. You can have different ideas from everyone else, if you want to—though why you want to is more than I can say. Just go to Mass, obey the laws, and worship God the way you think is best at home, in secret. Then you can live a normal life without being hunted to death wherever you go. You have no idea how much you have hurt your old aunt by turning your back on all you have ever been taught."

Margriete's eyes filled with tears. "Oh, Aunt Esta! I would never hurt you purposefully, unless I must to obey God's Word."

"Margriete!" Esta pled. "Look at what you are giving up. Just look at our beautiful Friesland"—she gestured out the open door to the autumn landscape—"where you could soon have your own home and family. You could live and die in peace. If you keep on like this, you will waste your life as a hunted outlaw, always in fear of your life."

Margriete followed her aunt's motion to the beautiful vista outside the cottage door. Fall flowers bloomed in thick profusion, and a few golden leaves were wafting down from the trees. High up in a branch, a songbird sang merrily, and Margriete thought again of her hopes and dreams of the future—dreams that she had given up on that unforgettable early morning a few months before. Could it be possible that she was wrong? Was she making a mistake after all?

Silence hung over the two like a heavy cloud. Aunt Esta waited expectantly.

"I knew what I was giving up before I joined the Doopsgezinde, Aunt," Margriete answered at last, dropping her eyes for an instant and raising them again. "I struggled long and hard before I made that decision. But now I have peace and joy such as I never knew existed.

"Even in prisons, souls are free. And, Aunt Esta…the joys of following God are worth dying for." Serene determination shone in Margriete's eyes. She searched her aunt's face eagerly, but Esta's eyes grew frosty, and there was a tinge of irritation there.

"Margriete, don't speak to me about these things anymore. At least I have done my part in warning you. All your relatives are loyal Catholics. Why do you have to disgrace your family and bring suspicion on us all?"

Margriete did not reply, because, really, she did not know what to say. *Nothing I say will convince her,* she thought silently. *Why try and make her angrier?*

Esta stood at the doorway and watched her niece leave. She was a mystery. It was unimaginable that a sweet girl like Margriete could give up her happy prospects for her future! Yes, Margriete certainly had changed.

The walk home was long for Margriete, and tears blurred her eyes as she followed the familiar path. She wondered what her aunt was thinking—not very flattering thoughts, she was sure. The family had been close-knit; Margriete was considered a humiliation, and she knew it. The realization hurt like no weapon ever could have.

Suddenly she was jerked out of her reverie by the distinct feeling of someone staring at her. She turned; sure enough, young Jan van Aernem was standing in the door of the blacksmith's shop. He made no attempt to hide his scornful glare, his black eyes seeming to burn holes in Margriete's clothing as she passed. "Heretic!" he spat, just loudly enough for the girl to hear. Margriete was shocked by the venom in his voice.

• • • • •

Two years flew by. Margriete was now nineteen and maturing in body and faith. Many were the hours that she had spent studying with Grietje and other sisters in the faith. How she loved to gather with them; they seemed almost as dear as her own family.

It was almost dark as Margriete slipped through the streets of Dokkum. She shivered a little. Autumn's coolness had set in quickly with the departure of the sun; however, Margriete felt a strange sense of foreboding this evening as she hurried to the illegal meeting in one of her neighbors' homes. "Lord, protect me this evening, if it is Your will," she breathed into the deepening darkness.

Silently Margriete walked to the back door of the cottage and knocked. Quickly she was recognized and pulled into the hushed conversation of her friends. "We must be extra careful tonight," Grietje whispered. "For some reason, the net seems to be tightening. I don't know how long this will go on undetected."

Margriete gasped. How could Grietje be so calm? Cold shivers of apprehension raced up her spine. Grietje squeezed her hand. "'If God is for us, who can be against us?'" she quoted softly as the two girls huddled together on the crowded bench. Margriete focused on the speaker, preaching to the tiny flock in the glow of the candle.

"A true Christian faith cannot be idle, but it changes, renews, sanctifies, justifies, and purifies more and more. It brings peace and joy. Happy is the person who has it and keeps it…to the end!" He opened a small copy of the forbidden Dutch Bible; in silence the little group listened to the inspiring words of Psalm 91. "He that dwelleth in the secret place of the most High shall abide under the shadow of the Almighty. I will say of the LORD, He is my refuge and my fortress: my God; in him will I trust.

"Surely he shall deliver thee from the snare of the fowler, and from the noisome pestilence. He shall cover thee with his feathers, and under his wings shalt thou trust: his truth shall be thy shield and buckler.

"Thou shalt not be afraid for the terror by night; nor for the arrow that flieth by day; nor for the pestilence that walketh in darkness; nor for the destruction that wasteth at noonday.

"Because thou hast made the LORD, which is my refuge, even the most High, thy habitation.... Because he hath set his love upon me, therefore will I deliver him: I will set him on high, because he hath known my name. He shall call upon me, and I will answer him: I will be with him in trouble; I will deliver him, and honor him. With long life will I satisfy him, and show him my—"

Suddenly the sound of a scuffle at the front door made Margriete's taut nerves tense in fear. Then there came a dreaded sound to the ears of the Anabaptists inside—loud pounding on the wooden door, with a vehement "Open!"

Margriete was seized with a wild desire to flee. Immediately the entire assembly was on their feet. Grietje had Margriete's hand and was pulling her toward the back door, facing the woods. "Quick!" Grietje whispered urgently. The pounding on the door was growing more forceful. The two girls fled out the door and directly into the path of a waiting soldier.

Chapter 11

Despair and Hope

Margriete shivered as she and Grietje huddled together on the bare stone floor of the tiny cell. Murky light filtered down between the bars far above them. Stunned and confined, the two girls took comfort in God and each other. They had known, of course, that this day might come, but who would have guessed that it could happen on such a tranquil, quiet evening?

Finally Grietje broke the silence with the first thing that came to her mind. "How did the authorities know that we were meeting tonight? We were so careful!"

Margriete sighed softly. "I don't know; but someone must have betrayed us. Someone who knew about the meeting and couldn't resist the reward of sharing information."

The girl thought of the angry glares the townspeople had thrown to the guards as the Anabaptists were being hauled toward prison. Most of them, she knew, were sympathetic, or at least respectful. For a moment the leering, mocking face of Jan van Aernem flashed into her consciousness. Could it be—?

Wearily Margriete shoved the thought out of her mind. She simply could not begin to suspect people. It wouldn't do any good now anyway. She could hear Grietje whispering to herself beside her. "'The Lord is my light and my salvation; whom shall I fear?'" Almost unconsciously, Margriete joined in. "'...Though a host should encamp against me, my heart will not fear; though war should rise against me, in this will I be confident...'"

The merry chirping of the sparrows in the bushes outside awoke Margriete from a restless sleep the next morning. She faced the day with dread as she thought of what was sure to come—the relentless questioning, the alternate pleading and threatening from the inquisitors. Several times, as she remembered a letter from prison detailing the ruthless inquisition that had circulated through Dokkum, her heart would clench in fear. Was she strong enough? Could she stand against their wily tactics?

But the day came and went with no sign of disturbance. So did the next day...and the next. For more than a week it was the same daily monotony, broken only by the sneers of the young guard who brought their daily ration of bread and water.

"Oh, Grietje!" Margriete moaned one day, dropping wearily to the hard, damp floor, "I am glad that we are so undisturbed, but this is hard to bear!"

"Margriete," Grietje said gently, "that is exactly what they—the Inquisition and the devil—want. They want us to become discouraged."

Margriete sighed, then she began to sing, remembering the song of the four men who had died at Enkhiuzen two years before. Sweet and clear, the pure notes rose out of the hopeless situation around them, joining the song of the birds in the freedom of the outside world. "I'd rather choose the sorrow sore,/And suffer as a child of God/Than have from Pharaoh all his store,/To revel in for one brief while…"

Prison life was hard on the two girls; neither was used to the coarse, scant food, rough handling, or hard, damp beds. Margriete grew thinner and her cheeks were less rosy. Grietje looked on in concern, but Margriete insisted that she was perfectly healthy.

Worse, perhaps, than the physical conditions, was the emotional strain. For three weeks Margriete kept her cheerful composure, but then one sunny afternoon, the rippling song of a bird bounced happily through the bars. Margriete rose in silence and walked to the window. Standing below it, she looked longingly up into the thin shaft of light that managed to filter in.

The song stopped; she turned away and sat down beside Grietje. Both were silent for a long time, then Margriete said, "Oh, Grietje, to think that I might never see my family again…" Margriete's voice trailed off, tight with tears.

Grietje reached over to her friend, and the two young prisoners embraced and wept for the hopes and promises and dreams that could never be theirs.

• • • • •

The day had come. Margriete was standing in a small room facing several black-robed men whose sole duty was to turn her back to the Mother Church.

"Who are you?" a small, dark man with sharp eyes began abruptly and almost mechanically.

She forced herself to look at him. "Margriete Emkens."

"How old are you?"

"Nineteen."

"Have you been rebaptized?" His eyes grew even sharper.

She paused. It was a life-or-death question. "Yes."

He was growing rapidly angrier, but continued firing questions. "Do you believe that Christ consecrates Himself, and is present in the bread? Christ said 'Take, eat, for this is my body;' and Paul said likewise."

Margriete ran her finger onto a knothole in the table. "Christ sitteth at the right hand of the Father; He does not come under men's teeth."

The questioner's sharp eyes flashed anger. "If you continue in this belief, you will have to go into the abyss of hell forever! It is what all heretics say." His voice softened and he leaned back a little in his chair. "Have pity on your youth. Look, your future is before you. Can you not give up these foolish ideas?"

For what seemed like hours the relentless interrogation went on. Most of the time their voices would be as smooth as fresh cream as they took advantage of Margriete's youth and hopes of the future, entreating her to save herself and recant. Yet she marveled at the grace of God as He put answers in her mind to the inquisitors' crafty questions and reasoning.

Finally Margriete was roughly escorted back to her cold, damp cell, where she prayed long and desperately for Grietje, who she knew was being subjected to the same treatment. She shuddered at the thought of Grietje denying her faith under the constant pressure. "Oh, Lord," she moaned into the decaying straw, "keep Grietje strong."

The days dragged by for Margriete and Grietje, and the increasingly cold nights made their damp beds more and more uncomfortable. Periodically one girl would be taken for sessions with the inquisitors, while the other waited in dread lest she would reject her faith.

"We ought to be thankful," Margriete commented wryly one cloudy afternoon, straining to see out the window. "Just imagine what we might be going through if we were middle-aged men."

Grietje shuddered at the bare thought. "They sure aren't above threatening us, though. They must have at least a little mercy on our age—and the fact that we are girls."

So far neither of the girls had been dragged to the infamous 'torture chamber' where the Inquisition used crueler means to persuade their prisoners. The whispered reports of what was likely to happen to you there was enough to make the most courageous man tremble. And always there was a nagging fear in the back of both girls' minds—*could I keep the faith, even there?* Rarely did they talk about it, but the tiny doubt was always present, like a dark, gray cloud hanging perpetually over their heads.

One of the bright spots for Grietje was that Margriete was teaching her to read. It was slow and she wished for books and real lessons, but she was making progress. Margriete's crude lessons scratched into the dust and dirt were very helpful, both in learning and making the days almost tolerable. Grietje had always wanted to be able to read.

Occasionally Grietje or Margriete would stand on tiptoe to peer out between the bars of the tiny window and report to the other on glimpses of the outside world. One day, as Margriete was straining her eyes to see the floating clouds, she gasped and her eyes widened in dismay and shock.

"What is it?" Grietje asked worriedly, jumping to her feet.

Margriete blinked. There was a young man walking in the prison courtyard, although he was obviously free, for he was conversing in very friendly tones with the burgomaster. Margriete's voice trembled a bit as she whispered, "It's Jan van Aernem."

The seed of suspicion that had been planted the evening they were jailed grew and darkened. She remembered all too clearly the hateful glances and spite-filled words that Jan had thrown at her every time she passed the blacksmith's shop. Could Jan have betrayed them?

Chapter 12

The Sword Christ Brought

M argriete, please!" Never had Margriete seen her father so agitated. "Your mother is distraught. She has hardly slept at all for weeks, and she is feeling terrible." His voice softened noticeably, but his eyes still glinted with determination. "Daughter, can't you just forget all this? Your younger siblings, especially Lijsken, are very bewildered and hardly know what to think, I can tell. Look at what you are doing to our family!"

He had chosen his subject carefully, and knew well the influence his words were sure to have on his sensitive daughter.

Tears welled up in Margriete's eyes and spilled out as she thought about her family. Vivid scenes flashed through her mind of the family playing, eating, and talking together. Had it been a hundred years ago?

"Oh, Father," Margriete said at last through her tears, "you don't understand. Christ is everything to me; how can I deny Him now, after all He has done for me?"

"Margriete, *you* don't understand," her father said sternly. Then lowering his voice, he went on, "Maybe these Anabaptists are right. I certainly don't agree with the Catholic Church, you know. It's just that there's no sense in my own daughter staying in prison for what she believes. Margriete, I have to admire your fortitude, but it's not necessary! Just come home, tell them you will be loyal, and go to Mass."

The father drummed his fingers rapidly against the wall. "If you still want to hold these ideas at home, I don't mind. No one will—except your mother, perhaps. You won't be in trouble and fear anymore, and you can live a normal life." A fatherly smile spread over his face. *"And*—get married and give me a few grandchildren."

Margriete blushed and twisted her hands in her apron. "But that would be deceiving people. And besides, I could never promise to be loyal to the Catholic Church, or go to Mass."

The smile vanished; the beginnings of anger took its place. "Listen to me, Daughter! You don't know what will happen to you if you don't do as I say. They"—he cast a hateful glance to the barred door—"have been lenient because of your age, but their patience never holds out for long. You will be sorry!" The ominous import of these words hung in the air for a long, painful moment.

A sudden rattling at the door indicated the jailer coming to let her father back out to freedom. As the door swung open, he hesitated and looked at Margriete, a world of pleading in his eyes. Speaking any more was not acceptable, but he made a slight motion toward the door.

Silently Margriete shook her head. After the sound of his footsteps in the cold hall died away, she dropped into the musty straw and buried her head in her hands, and tears trickled out between her fingers. Helplessly, Grietje looked on, and finally she reached over and laid her hand on Margriete's knee.

Margriete looked up finally and whispered, "'For it was not an enemy that reproached me; then I could have borne it: neither was it he that hated me...then I would have hid myself from him: But it was thou, my guide, and mine friend!'"

· · · · ·

The familiar sound of keys rattling in the lock jolted both girls awake the next morning. It was the usual supply of bread and water for the day, but Margriete was surprised to see that this was not the usual guard that seemed to take an evil pleasure in sneering at them every chance he had. This man was older, and instead of a mocking grin, his expression held a mysterious aura. Margriete's eyebrows lifted a little, but she pretended not to notice and averted her eyes.

Quickly the man set down their rations, then, in one swift motion, he jerked something out of a deep inner pocket, tossed it at them, and was gone without a word.

"What is this?" Margriete asked in surprise as she snatched it up. Then she gasped. "Grietje! Letters from home—from our families! And paper and a pen to reply!" She shoved a scrap of paper into Grietje's bewildered hands and unfolded hers. It was written in Lijsken's flowing hand.

Dear Margriete,

We miss you very much. Mother is so worried about you that she can hardly think about anything else. Can't you appease them some way? Then maybe they will release you. Janneken says to tell you that she wants you back home very, very much. We all do.

Father says to tell you to please forget that foolishness so that you will be set free. All the little ones cry for you. Please, Margriete, do what they tell you to. It is so terrible here; I don't believe anyone talks or thinks about much else. The townspeople are unhappy about the young people in prison; they do not think it is right. There is much angry talk about who might have betrayed you. Jan van Aernem actually admitted to it, which was a mistake. Everyone hates him now.

We love you and hope to see you again soon. Mother and I pray for you often.

Your loving sister,

Lijsken

For a long time Margriete sat gazing at the sheet of paper in her hands.

Jan… So he *had* betrayed them. She tried to forget, but it was hard when the consequences of his treachery faced her every second, waking or sleeping.

She thought again of her family, and tried to picture each one in her mind. She could imagine them sitting at the smooth table, discussing each sentence written, dictating the letter to Lijsken. Would she ever see them again?

With trembling fingers, she reached for the clean paper and

spread it carefully out on a smooth stone. Slowly she began to write.

> To my dear family:
>
> It was good to hear from you. I pray for you very much. Tell Grietje's family that she and I are both well and are confined together, for which we are very grateful to God. We are both still of the same mind and I am determined, by the Savior's grace, to keep the holy faith until death.
>
> Lijsken, I miss you. Keep the commandments of God, love that which is good, and it will go well with your soul. For you see, I am not imprisoned for murder or theft or any crime at all, except that of possessing the Word of God and following its precepts...

Chapter 13

The Trial

It was another round of the now-familiar questioning. However, this time, it was different.

Today it would be decided whether Margriete and Grietje would stay in prison or be released. Today it would be decided whether they would live or die. Today was their trial—a hypocritical one, to be sure, but their trial none the less. Soon the days and weeks and months of suspense would be over.

Spring had come; the sparrows were whistling shrilly and the leaves were unfolding and turning green. They had been in prison for five long, cold months, but the difficult winter ended at last.

Margriete and Grietje knelt together on the hard stone floor, imploring for strength and grace from the only One who could give it. And then, almost silently, they quoted in unison, "'Fear none of those things which thou shalt suffer: behold, the devil shall cast some of you into prison, that ye may be tried; and ye shall have tribulation...be thou faithful unto death, and I will give thee a crown of life!'"

Soon after the first bright rays of morning sifted into the cell, the girls were escorted roughly down the dank corridor together. Margriete was glad that so far they had at least had each other's company in their little cell. This was the first time, though, that they were to be questioned together.

A brooding, menacing silence hung over the room as Margriete and Grietje were shoved inside and roughly seated on crude chairs at a smooth table, opposite their opponents. Margriete noticed with dread that the sharp-eyed inquisitor of the first 'session' was directly across from her, and he regarded her with the cool glare of a panther eyeing its prey.

The usual questions were fired in monotonous succession. Then the questioners got down to the business of the day. The clerk held a pen poised over the paper.

"Did you not receive a baptism in your infancy?"

Margriete sighed inwardly. She had been asked this question at least a dozen times before. "I have no remembrance of what was done in my infancy: my parents told me that I was; but this was not in accordance to the Scriptures."

"But you have besides this received something more." His voice was smug.

"I have received one baptism that was according to the Word of God."

The questioner rubbed his hands together. "Do you not consider the baptism good that you received in your infancy?"

Margriete shifted her wrists in the tight cords. "If I had

considered it good, and a baptism, I would not have received another."

A glint entered his eye. "Who baptized you?"

"I cannot tell you." Margriete's voice was quiet, but firm. She knew that they could probably guess, but her admittance would make it worse for Menno, if he ever was caught.

"We have ways that will make you tell!" His voice carried an ominous and unveiled threat. Margriete kept silent.

Another man interrupted, "Margriete, it will go hard for you if you do not confess your error, and return to the Holy Roman Church."

Margriete shook her head slightly. "If you can show me my error according to the Word of God, I will gladly confess."

At this, the subject was abruptly changed. "Were you never at a meeting before you received baptism?"

"Yes, three or four times, at least."

He nodded in satisfaction. "Where were they held? In what houses?"

She clasped her fingers nervously. "Some were held in the woods."

"Where were the others?" He leaned forward in the chair.

Margriete lowered her eyes. "I cannot tell you."

At this another inquisitor cut in. "Margriete, we do not seek to see you suffer in the least; we pity your youth and your inexperience. You are young, and you have been led astray; think of your family and your future, and confess."

She raised her eyes to meet his. "I have told you that if you show me my error according to the Scriptures, I will confess."

Silence fell for a second. The clerk's quill was the only sound, recording all that Margriete had said. The sharp-eyed inquisitor picked up the papers and scrutinized them carefully.

He raised his eyebrows at Margriete and smiled a sympathetic-looking smile, but his eyes glittered cruelly. "Margriete, do you regret anything that you've said? We will gladly change it and forgive you of that statement."

A slight smile lingered on her lips. "You need not change anything."

A tall man sitting against the stone wall whispered to his companion in admiration, "Amazing! Have you ever seen someone so young be so sure of what she believes? Poor girl, she is far too delicate to waste away in a dungeon."

"It's her own choice," was the grim reply. "She could be released anytime she wished if she would recant."

"She won't be wasting away much longer, I'll warrant," an old man interjected, pity in his tones. "Those inquisitors are losing all patience, it seems."

Silently Margriete sat by as Grietje was subjected to much the same questions and pleadings and threatening. Then there was nothing to do but wait for the sentence to be read. The men in the room mocked and sneered at the two girls to their hearts' content.

Finally, after what seemed like hours to Margriete and Grietje, the clerk emerged from the tiny room, followed by the inquisitors, judges, burgomaster, and bailiff. The room immediately fell as silent as death. The clerk cleared his throat and pronounced solemnly,

"Whereas Margriete Emkens, daughter of Claes, of Dokkum; and Grietje Jans, daughter of Gijsbert, also of Dokkum, have been rebaptized and have joined the sect and heresy of the Anabaptists, holding pernicious views with regard to the sacraments of the holy Church, contrary to the holy Christian faith, the ordinances of said holy Church, and the written laws and decrees of her Imperial Majesty, our gracious lady; and, moreover, obstinately persist in their unbelief, errors, and heresies; therefore my lords the judges, having heard the demand made by my lord the bailiff concerning said persons, together with their confession, and having considered the circumstances of said case, condemn said persons to be drowned by the executioner.

So pronounced and ordered, this fourth day of April, 1543."

A heavy silence ruled in the courtroom. A few of the men looked shocked at the harsh sentence for two girls just into the bloom of young womanhood.

Grietje and Margriete were promptly separated and escorted to different cells, where neither knew what was happening to the other. Margriete glanced around her cell, which looked much like the one she had just left. *How can I know if Grietje keeps the faith?* she thought. *Oh, Lord, Lord, keep Grietje close to You!*

Margriete would be in prison for only five more days.

Chapter 14

Escape?

One day had passed since the trial and sentence—the longest, dreariest day Margriete had ever spent. And now, as the long shadows of evening crept toward the prison, the girl dropped wearily into the straw. Fear threatened to choke her breath when she tried to pray.

Drowning! Death. It sounded so hard...so cold...so *final*. She would never marry, never know the joy of holding her newborn child, never watch her babies grow into beautiful young men and women. Never again would she walk the streets of Dokkum with Grietje, or milk the cow, or wash the dishes, or kiss her mother good night. Her secure world had been crushed; she was a condemned prisoner in Leeuwarden.

With shaking hands Margriete smoothed her hair. Was this

the last night she would spend on earth? She glanced up toward the window, but angry clouds blanketed the moon and stars.

Tears pooled slowly in the corners of her eyes as she thought of all her shattered dreams, lying like smoldering ashes in the recesses of her soul. "O Lord," the girl moaned aloud, drawing her knees up to her chin and wrapping her arms around them, "I *want* to submit to You, but it is so…hard…"

For more than an hour Margriete sat alone, fighting with herself, her dreams, her desires. Only the cold stone walls were there to witness the fierce battle raging in her spirit. *Die…* before she was even twenty years old? Was she making the right decision? Could it…could it be that she really was wrong after all?

Slowly the girl slid to her knees and clasped her hands. Tears squeezed slowly out of her eyes, and her lips moved in the silent agony of her heart.

After a long time, with a new peace on her countenance, Margriete curled up on the floor and closed her eyes. New dreams, heavenly dreams, soothed her silent slumber.

And far above, the moon was shining again.

• • • • •

Grietje jerked suddenly awake from a fitful sleep. She sat up slowly, trying to still the wild pounding of her heart. There! It was a faint scratching coming from the locked door. Then a soft click. Tiptoeing footsteps moved away down the hall outside.

As if in a dream, Grietje slowly got to her feet and tiptoed toward the door. Silently she felt for the latch. It had been unlocked!

Slowly, so as to not make any noise, Grietje picked up her bonnet and pulled it close around her face. She tied her apron with fumbling fingers and gave the door a gentle push. It yielded easily. The girl pushed gently until there was a narrow opening and slipped out into the hall.

She had been well-educated by her long stay in prison. Without hesitation Grietje found her way through the maze of darkened halls. She looked at the door leading to freedom. It had been pushed half open to allow the sleeping guard the fresh April air. Like a shadow the girl fled into the shadows outside.

Quickly Grietje turned right and began to run—out of Leeuwarden, toward Dokkum and her family. She ran in the soft grass beside the street instead of on the noisy cobbles. By the height of the moon in the clear sky, Grietje judged it to be around one o'clock in the morning. She would have to hurry to get to Dokkum by morning.

As soon as the eastern sky began to lighten, Grietje detoured into the forest. She knew that the authorities would stop at nothing to get her back. Silently she picked her way through the brush, trying to step on moss or dirt instead of the crackly, dry leaves.

The sun was almost at full radiance by the time Grietje arrived in Dokkum. She crept to the edge of the woods, darted across the clearing to her home, and gave a few swift taps on the back door.

Then her family was all around her, laughing and crying and talking at the same time, while Grietje vainly tried to quiet them. The children sat wide-eyed and breathless while Grietje told her story, and her mother collapsed into a chair and cried with relief.

"Listen," Grietje said, retying her apron strings, "I must go now. This is the first place that will be searched. Don't ask where I'm going. It's safer that way."

"But what about Margriete?"

Grietje's eyes filled with unbidden tears. "She's still in prison, as far as I know, under sentence. I don't know which cell they put her in, or I would have tried to get a message to her. Really, I have no idea who unlocked my door. Maybe they unlocked hers, too. That would be much more dangerous, though. Someone might 'forget' to lock one door, but two would make it obviously intentional."

Grietje's mother had been flying nervously around the kitchen. She held out a small basket to Grietje. "Here, a little cheese and bread for you, in case you don't find shelter right away."

Grietje embraced her mother. "I love you, Father and Mother and all of you. I'll try to send word to you often." Then she turned and ran into the brightening day.

Chapter 15

The Crown of Life

Margriete scratched another small mark on the wall with a broken stick. She knew it was no use to count the days, but somehow it seemed strangely important to keep track of time. There were five faint marks on the stone now—*five days,* Margriete thought, *since I was sentenced. Perhaps Grietje has already been taken.*

Not a day had gone by that Margriete had not thought of Grietje, and prayed often for her. What if Grietje had given up? Margriete shuddered at the thought.

When the sun was beginning to peek into the window, Margriete began to listen expectantly for the 'bread boy' to bring her bread and water. She didn't really care about the tasteless food, but it was the only break in the endless monotony of prison life.

The sun slowly inched upward in the sky, and still the boy had not come. Silently, fear squeezed Margriete's heart—did they intend to starve her into submission? Anxiously she eyed the knob. Several hours had passed since the usual time.

Suddenly Margriete jumped at the sound of a familiar rattling at the door. But instead of a bucket and loaf being shoved in, two strange guards appeared and motioned for her to come.

Slowly the girl stood up and walked toward them. This must be the day that had been chosen. Why else would she be needed?

She held out her hands and they tied them tightly together. The guards were almost gentle in their handling of her as she breathed pure air and felt the sun's tender rays on her face for the first time in months.

Two other men joined them as she was led toward the canal, and kept up a steady monologue, trying to convince her to turn from her 'foolishness'. Margriete ignored them as if they were not there and glimpsed the canal's reflective ripples. It had suddenly lost all of its former beauty. How dark and brooding its murky waters looked! Her glance turned to the sky and held there, and peace came again.

• • • • •

Grietje crept silently along in the shadowy woods, being careful to keep out of sight of the road. She had learned a day before from a sympathetic townswoman when a young Anabaptist girl was to die, and could not bring herself to stray far away from Dokkum.

My poor family probably thinks I'm in Utrecht by now, Grietje thought sadly, stepping over a protruding rock. Grietje had taken care not to disclose her identity to anyone, and had not even gone back to her family in the four days since she had escaped.

The authorities were still in an uproar. How glad she was for the newly budded leaves that hid her stealthy movements toward the canal! Silently she slipped between overhanging branches and ducked under swaying vines.

Suddenly her heart leaped into her throat and she jerked to a stop. People were gathering along a wider area in the canal, spreading slowly along the banks, craning their necks to see.

Grietje found a small rock and stood on top of it, half-hidden by the thick trunk of a tree. She was about fifty feet away from the edge of the canal, and she strained her eyes to catch a glimpse of her friend. Tears blurred her eyes and the scene swam before her as she saw Margriete being herded between the crowd toward a small platform at the edge of the river.

Men and women began to stir about and murmur angrily. Such a young, beautiful girl…sweet-looking, too! Surely she did not deserve this! Grietje thought she saw one man clench his fists and open his mouth as if to speak, but a woman at his side silenced him with fear in her eyes. The inquisitors were sure to take swift and furious action toward any bold enough to protest.

A seventeen-year-old Swiss boy with dark eyes watched the scene intently. His gaze wandered to the girl's face, and at the same instant, her sweeping eyes caught him. And then Margriete smiled, a gentle, sweet smile that transformed her face. Her lips moved in the words, *I forgive you.*

She forgives me! Any kind of brutal satisfaction he might have derived from his treachery was swept abruptly away by that quiet forgiveness. The full, condemning force of what his betrayal had cost many people struck him suddenly, and shame crossed his face for a moment, but it did not linger. A curse to the Catholic Church, these Anabaptists! He set his teeth bitterly and walked sullenly away.

The inquisitors were clearly angry at the attitude of the people and anxious to show them who was in authority. Quickly they took the girl by the arms, but then hesitated as if to give her one last chance to return to the Roman Church.

But a clear, sweet voice rose out over the shocked and silent crowd from the rough platform, "'When this corruptible shall have put on incorruption, and this mortal shall have put on immortality, then shall be brought to pass the saying that is written, Death is swallowed up in victory.

"'O death, where is thy sting? O grave, where is thy victory?

"'Thanks be to God, which giveth us the victory through our Lord Jesus Christ!'"

Chapter 16

A House, a Man, a Story

The sky was a clear, azure blue, hanging like an infinite dome over the small town of Dokkum, Friesland. The gentle breezes of spring were waking the flowers and leaves from their long winter slumber, and along the dusty road leading out of the town, it seemed that the whole earth was vibrating with life.

An unnatural and muffled crackling sound drifted to the road from the woods, then stopped. Silence reigned for a few seconds, and then suddenly Grietje crept out of the leafy shadows.

"Where will I sleep tonight?" she murmured aloud.

The flaming sun was sinking lower toward the horizon before Grietje slowed her hasty walk. She stopped for a few seconds and considered; several hundred feet away stood a tiny but comfortable-looking cottage, well-kept and with vines flowering around its door, and a small barn nestled beside it.

Did she dare ask for lodging for the night? The slight girl glanced at the darkening horizon and felt the cooling air and the dew beginning to form, then she shook her head and walked firmly up to the house and knocked.

Several breathless moments passed, then a blonde young woman, stocky and smiling, answered the door.

Grietje was unused to asking for favors from strangers, and at that moment her voice and bubbly disposition suddenly failed her. "Hello," she faltered at last. "Would you be so kind as to let me sleep in your barn tonight?"

The woman flung open the door. "In our barn, no; in our house, yes. Come in!"

Grietje hesitated, blushed, and then stepped into the inviting kitchen. The hostess sized her guest up frankly, observing her serene face, her neat but dusty dress and apron, her unusually black wavy hair, and her dark eyes. The woman's friendly brow furrowed and she opened her mouth as if to speak, then thought better of it and turned back to her hearth.

"I hope I'm not intruding on you," Grietje said politely to break the strained silence, seating herself gratefully on the offered chair.

"No, no, not at all," the woman reassured her. "We have quite a few travelers stop here for the night—since we're so out of the way and all." Her merry laughter bubbled over the soup pot. "My name is Soetgen Munstdorp, but people call

78

me Soet." She paused, and Grietje knew that Soetgen was expecting her guest to introduce herself.

Grietje fingered her apron tensely. To let this woman know who she was would put both of them in danger. Should she take an assumed name or ignore the unspoken question? Grietje decided to overlook it.

"Do you live here alone?" the girl asked quickly, glancing around the room. Anything to turn the attention off herself.

"Oh, no," Soet said hastily, color deepening her face. "My husband, Claes, should be coming soon. There he comes now," she added with a hasty glance out the window.

Grietje waited nervously. How would this woman's husband react to this unknown and unexpected guest? He filled the door, a sturdy, sandy-haired peasant, with crinkles around his eyes and a smile at the corners of his mouth as he greeted his young wife. It was several minutes before he noticed the bright-eyed girl in the corner.

Soet quickly explained and introduced Grietje as best she could without asking her name. Grietje thought she detected a sort of amused, knowing glimmer around Soet's eyes. The man looked at her curiously, scrutinized her much as his wife had, but, to Grietje's relief, asked no questions.

"Quite an event at Dokkum today," he informed Soet between bites of food. "A girl, she looked about the age of our visitor here," waving his hand at Grietje, "was drowned in the canal. She was an Anabaptist, they say, but she was so young. That's why it made such a stir.

"She was well-known, too, a little shy, but sweet and intelligent, according to a woman who was standing there. Poor girl. I didn't have time to stay to watch it through, and I'm glad I didn't. But I had to stop and have a good look. She was slender, had curly blonde hair, and a delicate face.

"Remarkably calm for knowing that she only had a few minutes to live, too. It was very, very unusual. You know a lot of the townspeople, Soet. It could have been someone you knew."

"Didn't you think to ask her name?" Soet commented impatiently, spooning more soup into her bowl. "It's not every day that a young girl is drowned in a neighboring village—the village that *I* grew up in."

Her husband gulped some water before answering. "Just her first name—Margriete or something, I think. What does it matter? Oh, there was a girl imprisoned with her, one of her close friends, also an Anabaptist, that escaped several days ago. She would probably have been drowned too if they had been able to keep her locked up.

"Anyway, there's a reward on her head. Dark hair and eyes, they said, about nineteen years old, slim, probably wearing a blue dress and white apron." He threw a strange glance at his smiling wife, then at Grietje, leaving her to wonder and doubt in half-fear, half-amusement.

Did he *know* that the escaped girl was sitting across from him at his dinner table?

Chapter 17

Fleeing Southward

The sun had barely risen when Grietje left Soet and Claes's house and started southward again. She smiled a little to herself as she remembered her host's puzzled looks that he had thrown her all evening. He suspected her identity, she knew, but he would not betray her, would he? The best time to have done that would have been the night before, when she was asleep. Still, Grietje tried to distance herself from the hut as quickly as possible.

The girl sighed as she thought of Margriete. After escaping from prison several days before, her love for Margriete had kept Grietje from fleeing from Dokkum; she desperately wanted to know what her friend's fate would be. The faint hope that perhaps she would escape also and the two friends could travel southward together had been cruelly dashed.

They would never walk together on earth again.

Grietje had not had time to think about anything other than distancing herself from the dangers in Dokkum, but now she began to slow her pace and relax a little. She remembered her friend's victorious death and took refuge in a little grove of trees to grieve.

She thought of the first Anabaptist meeting they had dared to visit...Margriete reading the treasured Testament to her illiterate friend...their long imprisonment together...the endless interrogations...Margriete's pale but composed face as she faced her captors by the canal the day before...

Why had Grietje escaped and not Margriete? Why didn't the courageous person who 'forgot' to lock Grietje's door free Margriete instead? Vivid images of the brutal faces of the Catholic inquisitors glaring at the defenseless girl flashed into Grietje's troubled mind. Her face tensed and she bit her lip. Could she forgive these men who had killed her dearest friend and would have murdered her also?

Tears stung Grietje's eyes and she gazed unseeingly at her tightened fingers. Several long, painful moments passed, and then the friendless girl dropped to her knees in the grass.

• • • • •

The sound of horses rapidly approaching startled Grietje out of her intercessions heavenward. The sound was coming from the direction of Dokkum. *They may be looking for me,* she thought, shivering. But she couldn't just stand here in the field trembling, or they would surely recognize her at once.

Quickly she jerked her bonnet over her hair so it would

shade her face, shook out her apron and began trudging slowly back northward along the road just as the small party rounded the bend.

They were coming at a fast clip, the horses' showy trappings gleaming in the clear morning sun. There were four of them, Grietje noticed, obviously looking for someone.

"Good morning, girl," one of them shouted gruffly, looking as though he thought it was anything but good. "Have you seen a young woman—dark hair and eyes—heading south on this road?"

"No," Grietje replied softly, not raising her eyes and hoping they did not recognize the fear in her voice. Well, she hadn't seen anyone! *Lord, don't open their eyes,* she pled silently.

"Come on," one of the men said impatiently. "She's just a simple peasant. She probably couldn't even tell us that the sun rises in the east." With a noisy jingle of bridles, they were trotting off and away from Grietjie.

Grietje breathed a sigh of relief, but she continued retracing her steps, heading back toward Dokkum. She could not run the risk of the men returning and finding her walking south again. As soon as they were out of sight, she took to the shelter of the woods and turned her face toward South Holland once more.

Chapter 18

A Martyr's Letter, a Dying Request

Utrecht was a busy and bustling city, teeming with life. Birds twittered happily in the spring breeze and the scent of early roses lingered in the air. Children shouted and laughed in the streets, and men and women hurried here and there on unknown errands of the day.

Grietje forced herself to move naturally, to walk along the road as if she were quite at home in Utrecht, but inwardly she wondered how to find refuge without attracting suspicion. Opposition against the enemies of the Catholic Church was stronger in the South, she knew, and her only hope of protection lay in the fact that she was a stranger. And in a large city like Utrecht, a young girl would not be noticed, would she?

The only thing that had convinced her to enter this city was that there were friends there. Grietje hated to ask complete strangers for shelter, and desperately needed trusted companionship.

Carefully following her mother's hasty instructions, she wound her way through the dusty streets and up to a small board house sandwiched between several others of similar construction. Cautiously she counted four homes from the corner, then walked up to the sturdy door and knocked. Almost immediately a woman's voice called out, "Come in."

Cautiously Grietje pulled open the door. The home was rather bare and dim, but it was clean and warm, and a woman was sitting on a chair in the corner, reading. She had, Grietje noticed with hope, eyes with a marked resemblance to her mother's. Her hair, graying but still thick, was pulled back loosely from her open face under a white cap.

"Good day," Grietje said courteously, her bright smile flashing across her face. "Are you Mrs. Dorcas van Rijn?"

"Yes," the woman answered softly, a spark of curiosity leaping into her brown eyes. "And who are you?"

Grietje laughed a soft little giggle. "I'm Grietje Jans, from Dokkum in Friesland. My mother, Esther, is your second cousin."

"Esther!" Dorcas was genuinely shocked. "I didn't know she had a daughter your age. How old are you? Eighteen? Nineteen? And—" her voice dropped to a mere whisper, "a sister in Christ?"

"Nineteen, and yes, I am," Grietje replied, a glad smile illuminating her face. And then she told the woman her story—of Margriete, of her escape, her family, and news from Dokkum. Dorcas listened, sometimes smiling, sometimes laughing, sometimes crying.

"Are you in danger here?" Grietje inquired finally.

"Yes," Dorcas replied promptly, her face sobering. "Your magistrates could almost be called tolerant compared to ours. If your friend Margriete had been captured here, she would probably not have been drowned; she would have been burned, maybe alive."

Grietje shuddered. If she was arrested, that could be her fate, she knew. Had she been a fool to come? Would she have been safer on the other side of the Zuiderzee?

• • • • •

Six weeks passed uneventfully, with Grietje staying in Dorcas's house and out of sight as much as possible. But one dreary afternoon, when she stepped outside to get a little fresh air, a hand grasped her shoulder from behind and a man's voice whispered in her ear, "Are you Grietje Jans?"

Grietje's first impulse was to tear away from the unknown grip and flee. But where? A running, strange girl would be easily noticed in Utrecht. With fear squeezing her heart, she turned slowly around and said, "Yes, I am."

It was a young man with sandy hair and blue eyes, and his face was gentle, almost amused. Grietje relaxed a little.

"I was told to give you this," he said abruptly, shoving a small package into her hand. Then he turned and vanished into the sidewalks and alleys of Utrecht. Grietje was aware that the underground church had a fairly sophisticated system of communication, but she was still very surprised. What was this?

Grietje walked slowly into the house, fingering the edges of the white envelope. It was unmarked; there was not even a smudge to give a hint to the writer's identity. She shoved it into her pocket and entered the house. "Dorcas, can you read?"

"Why, yes," she answered. "Why?"

Grietje handed her the package. "I think it's a letter. Can you help me read it?"

Dorcas opened it carefully. "Why, Grietje, there are two letters, but something is strange. This one looks old, as though it hasn't been opened for years."

As Grietje leaned closer to look, she gasped and her face turned pale. "But what is this other note? Will you read it to me?"

Dorcas unfolded it slowly, smoothing out the creases, and began to read aloud.

> My Dear Grietje,
>
> We pray for you often and hope to hear from you soon. Everyone is missing you very much.
>
> I have sad news for you. Your friend Verena died suddenly three days ago. Several hours before she died, she gave me this—I think it's a letter of some sort—and said, 'Please give this to Grietje. I want her to have it. She knows all about it.'
>
> I don't know anything about it. What is going on, Grietje? May God bless you and keep you safe. Your brothers and sisters hope to see you again sometime soon.
>
> Much love,
>
> Your mother.

Dorcas looked at Grietje. "What is this, Daughter?"

Grietje was silent. Dorcas took Verena's letter gently in her hands and turned it over. The ink on the back was faded and worn, but she could still make out the words: To My Only Son.

"'My Only Son'?" Dorcas was thoroughly puzzled. "Grietje?"

Grietje smiled a little in spite of herself, but quickly sobered again. She sat silent for several long moments, and Dorcas looked up to see tears in her eyes. She reached over and touched the girl's clasped fingers gently, but said nothing.

Finally Grietje sighed and began to talk. Slowly she repeated the story that Verena had told, stopping only to answer Dorcas's eager questions.

"But why keep it a secret? Why not give the boy the letter?"

Dorcas was shocked to see Grietje burst into tears. "He has been raised to hate all enemies of the Catholic Church. How could he be persuaded that the letter is genuine with such an attitude?" Grietje bit her lip, and her face mirrored her grief. "And Dorcas…if it were not for that boy, Margriete would be alive today."

"But—"

Grietje straightened the pleats in her apron with shaking fingers. "Dorcas, he betrayed us, Margriete and me and several others. He even has boasted about it, it was whispered to me. Whether that is true, I don't know. But all of Dokkum is certain who is at fault that we were arrested. Oh, Dorcas—" Grietje stopped and covered her face with her hands, and tears trickled between her fingers. "I pray that God will help me to forgive him, but it is hard!"

And so the letter was tucked away onto a tiny shelf, the remnant of a mother's love, a seal almost two decades old, its contents still a mystery.

Chapter 19

But Not in Despair

The clouds were hanging low over Dokkum, threatening to burst in torrents of water. The damp streets were generally deserted, and through the windows of the small houses contented families could be seen enjoying the evening meal. The clammy smell of rain hung in the air and it seemed that even the birds were silent.

A young man shambled slowly up a narrow road, kicking viciously at unfortunate bits of pebbles. His face was set and he shook his head suddenly as if to clear it of troubling thoughts, then reached up and brushed his dark hair out of his eyes almost fiercely.

A door opened across from him, and a boy's voice called

out, "Good evening, Jan. Why are you out walking around tonight? More 'business' to do?" Harsh laughter bounced off the cobbles.

Jan turned silently away. The previous week's events had bothered him more than his pride would ever allow him to hint. Whenever he lay down to sleep, Margriete's sweet face rose before him, saying "I forgive you," as she had just before she died.

She was young, so young, just in the fresh bloom of womanhood. And yet, she had forgiven him... He was her murderer, and both of them had known it. What had he done? He was responsible for her death.

The townspeople had also turned against him. When Jan walked the streets or visited friends, he heard men and women hissing "Judas!" or "Traitor!" quietly, but with venom lacing their words; and children, catching their elders' spirit, mocked him openly. The common people had been moved by the sight of the defenseless girl in the hands of her rough enemies, and most of them had pitied Margriete and hated her betrayer.

Maybe I should just leave, he thought sullenly. *The people here detest me, the family I'm living with can't figure me out, my friends think something's wrong with me—bah! I could just run away. The van Aernems wouldn't miss me much.*

He kicked his foster family's door open and plodded back to the bedroom. Long after the rest of the family was asleep, Jan lay brooding. *I think I will go.*

He gathered clothes and food in the dark, piled them noiselessly into a basket, and slipped out the front door into the dreary night.

· · · · ·

Grietje sat quietly in the chair—unusual for the lively girl—with her chin cupped in her hand, gazing silently at the tiny window. Her eyes suddenly turned to the insignificant shelf in the corner, and she sat up straight and blinked.

"Dorcas?"

The woman turned toward her from where she had been bending over the fire. "What is it, Grietje?"

"Dorcas, how are we going to put that letter in Jan's hands? I can't go back to Dokkum for now, and—and, oh, Dorcas, the sight of it bothers me."

Dorcas sighed and sat down by the table. "I don't know. Do you think he would believe it's genuine? I mean, what proof would he have that it's not a cruel trick on our part?"

"If only Verena was still alive." Grietje twisted her apron absentmindedly. "If only she had given it to him a year ago... but we have it now, and I don't know why, but it's hard for me to have it in the house. Please try to understand me, because I don't understand myself, Dorcas. I—I've chosen to forgive him, and that letter is his."

Dorcas tightened her lips thoughtfully. "Well, child, it's pretty well impossible to get it to him now. If he would show up in Utrecht...but that won't happen."

"I almost hope it doesn't," Grietje remarked.

• • • • •

Six months smiled upon the Netherlands in steady procession. The soft emerald of summer gave way to the brilliant tints of autumn. Grietje gradually settled into life in Utrecht and adjusted to 'living the life of a hunted rabbit' as she had commented to Dorcas. Dorcas had continued the reading lessons that Margriete had begun in prison. Her life was taking on a normalcy that she hadn't known for a while.

One cool, sunny day she asked suddenly, "Dorcas, do you think it's safe for me to attend a Doopsgezinde meeting in the city here?"

"No," Dorcas replied frankly, with a wry attempt at a smile. "It isn't and it never will be, as close as I can guess. But that doesn't mean that you can't go. We need fellowship, even if it is dangerous."

Grietje walked to the window. "Do you know where one will be held this Sunday?"

Dorcas picked up Jan's letter and replaced it again. "No, but I'll try to find out for you. I have some friends at the market."

That Sunday as Grietje set off toward the house indicated for a much-longed-for meeting with other believers, she remembered the many times that she and Margriete had done just this during the last several years in Dokkum. What sweet times they had had! What memories they had made!

Grietje rejoiced in the refreshing service. As the tiny congregation knelt for prayer, her mind flashed back to the last time she had attended a meeting like this—had it been an eon ago?—a year before, and how it had ended in disaster. Then she had been in her hometown, with her own relatives, but she had been captured, imprisoned, and sentenced to the fate which had become Margriete's.

Was she being a fool, after all, to imperil her life for what she believed? But no, the question was her soul, her eternal soul, which she had pledged forever to Christ her King. She could not turn back.

As Grietje rose from her knees, a pleasant-faced woman caught her eye. She was middle-aged, graying slightly, but her blue eyes were still clear and lively, with creases at their edges that crinkled when she smiled. Something about her reminded Grietje of her mother—maybe it was the tender look in her eyes when she glanced at her children.

When the people were dispersing to leave, Grietje walked up to her. "Hello," Grietje said, smiling. "I'm Grietje Jans."

"And I am Levina, visiting here from Ghent," the woman replied, her eyes twinkling but quickly growing sober. "And please don't ask my last name. It's safer that way. If you're questioned, for all you know it's the wrong Levina."

"Is it that bad there?" Grietje was startled.

"Indeed, child, it is, and it's getting worse every day. I never know but what I may be the next one arrested, but God gives grace. I have six children"—she waved her hand at two lively boys. "There are a few of them, and the rest stayed home. I'll leave tomorrow afternoon to go back to Ghent."

Curiosity overtook Grietje; she wanted the answers to her questions. "What is the people's attitude toward us in Ghent?"

Levina sighed. "I really don't know. They don't dare to be openly sympathetic, if they are. Some, of course, are blatantly hostile, but most are rather indifferent, it seems to me. The men whose duty it is to track us down are much more diligent here than in the North, I've heard. Maybe it's just that the cities are larger in the South."

Chapter 20

At the Bread Shop

Frost glittered over the faded grass and turned the bare trees into delicate works of art. The canals were frozen to a slippery sheen and children shouted gleefully as they slid across them.

Grietje did not leave the house often, but today she felt desperately in need of fresh air and the freedom of the crisp, wintry city. Well, not quite freedom. Was it freedom when one was in constant fear of being hounded down and thrown into prison? But the girl was relatively unknown in Utrecht, and she decided to brave the streets. Dorcas reluctantly gave her consent for Grietje to buy the week's provisions and sent her off.

For close to a half hour Grietje meandered the street, purchased a few things, and snuggled them carefully down into the market basket on her arm. Finally, just a few hundred yards from home, she ducked into a small shop to buy a little bread.

A girl was there attending the tiny store, rosy and smiling, and Grietje felt the teenager's eyes boring into her while she selected a loaf. While Grietje was paying, the girl opened her mouth, closed it again, and finally decided to speak.

"Are you—are you—uh, do you happen to be an Anabaptist?"

Grietje was shocked. How did this young storekeeper know? Was the girl an informer? If she was, Grietje's answer could well cost her her life. But she had to run the risk.

"Yes."

"Oh, please don't leave. I'm Anneken, and please, I want to ask you some questions."

Fear shadowed Grietje's eyes. What proof did she have that Anneken was sincere? For all she knew, the girl had been hired to extract information from suspected Anabaptists. The silence in the room became almost oppressive before Grietje spoke. "But how did you know?"

Grietje looked into Anneken's eyes, and to her surprise, she saw tears there. "I can tell you don't believe that I'm in earnest," she said. "Oh, please believe me. You don't need to tell me your name. You aren't in danger then, are you? As for how I knew, it was something in your eyes. You…it reminded me—" she broke off suddenly and silence fell for a moment. "Well, you see—I know this is strange for me to talk like this to you, but I need someone, and I think I can trust you.

"I had an aunt, who was one of my favorite people. I was about seven years old at the time. Anyway, one day she took me aside and said, 'Anneken, I have to leave you, and you probably won't see me again. But I want to tell you this: when you grow up, remember your aunt and find the Anabaptists. They are the ones who worship God in spirit and in truth.'

"I knew she was in earnest, and I also knew that she was an Anabaptist, whatever that was. My family is very Catholic, but I never forgot what my aunt said. That happened eight years ago. And today I told God, 'Please let an Anabaptist come to our shop today. I can't stand this anymore.' And when you came in, I just thought I'd ask you."

Grietje was rather dazed, but she was thinking fast. The girl seemed sincere enough, but why on earth would she pour out her heart to someone she didn't even know? But Anneken knew now that Grietje was an Anabaptist, and that couldn't be helped anymore. Even if she was a spy, Grietje may as well answer her questions. So she said gently, "What did you want to know about us, Anneken?"

The girl picked up a loaf of bread and touched it thoughtfully. "I can't understand you people," Anneken blurted out. "Look, if I had been the wrong person, you may as well have been signing your own death warrant for just telling me that you are an Anabaptist like that. And I've seen it before. Why? Why don't you…. hedge or something? Aren't you afraid?"

Grietje paused. "Well, Anneken, I don't want to die, but I'm not afraid to die. Have you read the Bible?"

Anneken set the loaf down on the shelf. "No."

Grietje squeezed her eyes shut for an instant before continuing. "Well, Christ told His disciples that if they denied Him before men, He would deny them in heaven. This life doesn't count for much compared to eternity, does it? You see, all that a man can do to you is kill you, and then his power stops. You have to make the decisions about your soul. That's why people who are right with God don't have to fear death." An image of Margriete's composed face, shining with heavenly anticipation, flashed through Grietje's mind and her eyes grew soft.

Anneken shook her head. "But what about the magistrates and judges and bailiffs that do those things to you? It's terrible!" She lowered her voice. "Most of the townspeople here think so, I believe, but they're afraid to show it. Isn't it awful? How do you feel?"

Grietje sighed. Here was an area that she had fought long and hard in herself. "Christ told us to love our enemies, and pray for them that persecute us. We are told to do good to them and bless them, and we try to do that."

"I can't see how you do it." Anneken crinkled her forehead. "But I can tell that you believe what you say."

"Here," Grietje said impulsively, reaching into a pocket in her dress. "Can you read?"

Anneken held her thumb and forefinger about an inch apart. "A little."

Grietje held out the tiny leaflet. "I have a little book here, but it's forbidden. You understand what I mean? I've been saving it until I find someone who wants it and can read, because I can't read very well. But, if it's found in your possession, it could be prison, or worse, for you. Do you want it?"

Anneken took the tiny booklet, turned it over, and glanced at the title. *"The True Christian Faith,"* she murmured. She carefully turned over a few pages and read a sentence here and there. She sighed, twisted her apron, and considered, while Grietje prayed silently. "I'll take it," she said at last.

"All right, Anneken, and I'll pray for you," Grietje told her softly. "If you decide that you don't want it after all, you can give it back to me. Otherwise, you may keep it."

"Thank you....whatever your name is!" Anneken whispered. "Good-bye."

Grietje turned away thoughtfully. If the girl was a spy, Menno Simons' little booklet was palpable and incriminating evidence against her.

"Lord, keep me safe," she whispered into the windswept sky.

Chapter 21

A Disastrous Lord's Day

The sky was like a polished tin dome, thick gray clouds blanketing the January sun. Grietje was on her way to a Sunday morning meeting; since the weather had become colder, they usually met in homes. Grietje had melted easily into life at Utrecht and was learning to enjoy it, although she missed her family and friends in Dokkum.

"Don't you think it's quite dangerous?" Dorcas had come to love her sweet, talkative guest like a daughter.

"Remember what you told me a few weeks ago, Dorcas?"

Grietje's eyes twinkled. "I seem to recall that you told me it never will be safe, but we go anyway."

Dorcas drew a deep breath and sat down in a chair. "Go, then, Grietje, and God go with you. I'm just worried today, for some reason. Good-bye."

The girl turned toward the door. "Good-bye, Dorcas."

Grietje creased her dark brows. *Now I wonder why Dorcas is feeling like that. She has never behaved like this before.*

The home where the meeting was to be held was a little less than a mile away. Grietje covered the distance quickly, for the streets were still quiet in the thin light of early morning. Only a few families had gathered when the service began.

Close to ten o'clock, a boy burst unannounced through the closed door. The small group simultaneously turned toward him in surprise and fear. He was breathless from exertion, but managed to gasp out his message. "There are…soldiers coming toward this house…about a half mile away. They might…be coming for you!" Without another word, he disappeared out the door the way he had come.

A few of the women gasped, and children, sensing the tension, began to cry. Grietje clasped her hands in dread. Where would thirty people go on this cold, blustery day? But the host, a balding, middle-aged man, quickly took charge of the situation. "Women, girls, and children first. Go out the back door and disperse in different directions. Young men next, and hurry! As for us men, when you all are out of sight, we'll go too. Quick, everyone!"

Accordingly, Grietje slipped out with the women. She took a roundabout way home and told a startled Dorcas what had happened.

"Grietje," Dorcas announced gently, setting two cups on

the table, "I hate to say this, but I believe that maybe you should move on—maybe to Ghent. Things are getting dangerous here, and I don't know if the city authorities in Utrecht have been told about you or not."

Grietje sighed and looked at the closed door. "Don't you think I could go back home to Dokkum? I haven't seen my family for months. Is Ghent any safer than it is here?"

"Why don't you wait for five more months," Dorcas suggested. "Go down to Ghent—oh," her eyes brightened, "maybe Levina would let you live with her. And that letter. When you go back to Dokkum in the spring, perhaps you can take it along. Yes, Ghent is probably at least a little safer, because it's bigger than Utrecht and you're completely unknown there. Pray about it, Grietje, but you should leave soon."

Grietje prayed about it. That afternoon she retreated to her tiny bedroom and dropped to her knees. It was just that much farther from her home, her friends, her family—all that was close to her heart. Was there no end to constantly being hunted? What would it be like to be able to worship as she pleased, without fear? "O Lord," she whispered desperately, "please show me what to do."

The light was a little warmer when dawn lit the Netherlands the next day; thin icicles sparkled and dripped in the fresh morning sun and the world thawed and glittered.

"I suppose I'll leave you shortly," Grietje announced unexpectedly, setting her cap on her head. "To Ghent," she added, answering Dorcas's unspoken question. "Could you...could you write to Levina and ask her if I could stay with her? I'll sew or bake or do something to support myself. I hope I won't be a bother."

Tears sparkled in the corners of Dorcas's eyes, but she

managed a smile. "My dear child, you couldn't be a bother to anyone if you tried. And yes, I'll write the letter for you. You will wait until it's delivered and you have an answer?"

Grietje looked at the polished floor and her eyes sought for understanding. "It's, well, I guess it's hard for me to ask her myself." She smiled wryly. "I'm not used to begging for help…"

"*You* will be a blessing to *her*. Don't worry, Grietje."

•••••

Several long weeks later a warm reply was carried up to Utrecht with a trustworthy young businessman, welcoming Grietje to Levina's home.

Grietje set off two days after they received Levina's reply. "Thank you so much, Dorcas…you've done so much for me. And even teaching me how to read a little," her eyes flashed merrily, "even if I was rather dense. God bless you and protect you."

"And God be with you, Grietje. May you have a safe journey. Do be careful."

Grietje was walking the roads again, pushing southward toward Ghent. The trees' bare branches glistened in the glorious light, and the frozen blades of grass gleamed like threads of gold in the sunshine. Even though she glanced about warily in the afternoon light, Grietje admired the handiwork of God.

A shabbily dressed peasant boy came whistling toward her, but Grietje gave him no heed. She forced herself to act calm, to draw no attention to herself. In all her thoughts and fears of the future, the dark-haired girl slipping along the frozen road never dreamed of the grief and predicaments and tears that awaited her in the largest city of southern Holland.

Chapter 22

"For God Is My Salvation!"

1543 gave way to the fresh dawn of 1544 before Grietje reached her destination. Standing on the outskirts of Ghent, she paused and looked around her. Ghent was a large and bustling city, quite a bit bigger than Utrecht, with naked trees casting their delicate shadows on the ground and walls and homes. Hundreds of unknown faces were moving hither and thither on the dusty roads, and the cobbles clacked under her feet in the crisp air.

Levina had told her exactly where she lived in her letter to

Grietje, so the girl turned confidently down the narrow streets. Suddenly she stopped, craning her neck past the crowd. A forbidding stone building was seemingly thronged with people, and loud, angry voices rang out over the silent men and women, then muffled, much calmer answers. Grietje strained to understand the words, but they were meaningless; she was too far away.

Curiosity overtook her. It was unwise, she knew, but she pushed forward through the press until she was close to the door and could see inside.

Unexpectedly Grietje swayed and grasped the doorpost. "Levina!" she whispered.

It *was* Levina, and a young boy, perhaps sixteen, in the large room. Both were bound. The boy was being questioned loudly.

"Who are those people?" Grietje asked in an undertone to another young girl beside her. The girl looked at her closely. "Friesian?"

Grietje took a step backwards. "Yes."

The girl laughed quietly. "I could tell by your accent."

"But who—?"

"They're David van der Leyen and Levina Ghyselins," the girl replied, turning her attention back toward the prisoners. "This is rare—for their questionings to be here where people can see. Both of them are very well-known around here. Especially the boy. He's talented and extremely kind and intelligent. It seems that everyone appreciates him."

Grietje looked toward the front. She remembered when she and Margriete had been in that situation, and shuddered slightly.

"What do you think of the holy sacrament?" a noisy voice was echoing over the people. It was a priest, and his angry voice contrasted strangely to his religious array. He fingered his vestments while waiting for an answer.

"It is nothing less than idolatry," David replied quietly. He was standing only a few feet away from the sharp-eyed questioner, but his shoulders did not slump in defeat, as might be expected from a prisoner who had little hope of escaping with his life.

The priest shook his head. "Friend, you err greatly, that you so readily confess your faith, for it will cost you your life, if you do not change your mind."

David did not seem surprised by the threat. "I am ready to shed my blood for Jesus Christ, even now in this place; for God is my salvation, and He will keep me, and preserve me from all evil."

The man shook his head again in mock pity. "It will not be as good as though you were put to death secretly here in this place; but you will be burnt publicly, for an everlasting reproach." The voice was turning snappish. People stirred and whispered; everyone knew that it was not an idle threat.

Citizens strained their eyes in unison to see the prisoners' reaction, but David did not move. His back was erect, and he was steady and did not even blink. Levina started a little, but she did not lose her composure. "No one will ever be able to prove that the faith which I now die for is heresy," David said firmly, breaking the ominous silence.

Annoyed, the priest turned to Levina. "You have six children. Do you unfeelingly forget them and leave them to the mercy of others?"

Tears laced Levina's voice, and she glanced involuntarily in the direction of her home. "The Father will watch over my children, for He sees that I give them up for Christ."

Grietje turned away. She would go to Levina's house and see about the children. Fighting tears, she slipped away from the prison and found Levina's children crying in their kitchen.

What if the soldiers come back to take the children away? Grietje thought fearfully. *Will they arrest me too?* She pushed the thought out of her mind. *The children. They need someone to comfort them.*

The older boys stayed away warily from this strange young woman, but a little girl ran crying to her, desperately needing someone to cling to. Grietje picked the child up and hugged her. *You poor child, perhaps you will soon be motherless.*

A gentle knock at the door startled Grietje, and then a motherly woman and a shy girl, obviously people the children knew and trusted, stepped in and took charge of the situation. Grietje quietly slipped out of the house and began walking aimlessly down the bustling streets. She wandered the roads of Ghent dazedly until she came to a large square, crowded with people. There was a hastily erected platform in the center of the crowd, and two stout poles...and Levina, David, a priest, and several soldiers were standing on it.

David dropped suddenly to his knees and began to pray, but he was roughly jerked to his feet again and shoved toward the stakes. The crowd murmured.

A hush fell over the people. The two prisoners were escorted roughly to the two splintery posts. Men threw chains around them, fastening them on the opposite side of the post. The crowd watched their every movement, for many condemned criminals, reasoning that they had nothing to lose, fought with the viciousness and desperation of despair. But neither made any move to resist. David did not even look at the men binding him fast.

The soldiers straightened and walked away. A numbness swept over Grietje as lit torches were brought and straw and wood were piled around the stakes. She opened her mouth, but no sound came forth. *No, O Lord, no!*

Then David's voice rang out over the waiting men and women, and many leaned forward to catch his words. But he was speaking to Levina. "Rejoice, dear sister! for what we suffer here is not to be compared to the eternal glory that awaits us."

Levina was silent, but she smiled, a gentle smile that shone and looked strangely out of place in her cruel surroundings. The crowd shifted restlessly, and Grietje heard whispered snatches of indignant conversation. "…So young…and the woman—she has six small children…isn't he intelligent-looking? It's a shame!…shhh…they'll hear you… Look!"

At this, Grietje looked. A tiny bag of gunpowder was being tied to both Levina and David, and then the fires were kindled. Silence descended over Ghent; even the birds hushed their warbles. Almost in unison, the two doomed citizens lifted their eyes toward the azure sky and cried, "Father, into Thy hands we commend our spirits!"

"This is insanity!" a youthful merchant hissed to no one in particular, roughly stabbing a gaudy feather more firmly into his hat. "A young, handsome, talented boy and a middle-aged, defenseless mother. Who looks like true Christians to you?" "Shh…they'll hear you…what a ridiculous thing…despicable!… I agree with you…" The people of Ghent were not yet immune to human suffering.

Grietje fought tears and twisted her hands in her apron. "Oh, God, can't You see this wickedness? Why do You not do something?" her silent protest drifted to heaven. And a still small voice answered, "Many people are being influenced toward truth by this blatant iniquity today."

Three agonizing hours passed. Grietje thought of leaving, but her legs would not obey her. She felt fastened to the ground in horror and dread. Levina had long since gone to her reward, but the crowd lingered. Grietje stood numbly, gazing at the ground. She could not bring herself to lift her eyes toward the platform. Suddenly the crowd stirred excitedly. "Did you see that? He moved! David moved!…he lives!…he lives!…a miracle!"

Still Grietje did not look, fearing what she might see. Some men in the crowd shouted in protest. "The executioner stabbed him!…three times…poor boy!…what cruelty!…how awful…Look! He still moves!…incredible!…the executioner broke his neck…"

A woman screamed. Some looked deathly pale.

Silence. Deathly, agonizing silence. Then—"He is dead! He is dead!"

The throng revolted. Some threw stones. A few men shouted reproof and fury, then ducked quickly into the anonymity of the crowd. Girls fainted. Women moaned. Children shrieked.

Grietje turned away, fighting tears, her stomach tying itself into knots. "Father in heaven…where shall I go now?"

Chapter 23

Home!

There was nothing to do but leave the city. Levina had been the only person she knew in Ghent. Weeping, Grietje retraced her steps to the outskirts of Ghent and turned north. North, toward Friesland and Dokkum and *home*.

She had only walked for several hours when the sun began to dip toward the horizon and the air grew noticeably colder. Grietje shivered. She only had one other set of clothing besides what she was wearing, and that was certainly not enough to keep her warm if she was forced to sleep under the stars. Slowly Grietje veered off the road behind a thick clump of bushes and knelt on the frosty ground.

The forces of evil drew away, for the little circle of bushes and dry grass around the lonely girl had become a holy place.

. . . . .

Grietje traveled as quickly as possible for almost another hour, until the cold forced her to ask for shelter. "Why, yes," said a graying woman who answered her knock. "I live here by myself, and you are certainly welcome to spend the night. I'm Maeyken. And what is your name?"

Grietje hesitated. But she was a long way from home; surely she would not be recognized. "Grietje Jans," she answered with a dimpled smile. "Thank you for letting me stay with you."

"Where are you traveling from?" Maeyken inquired, turning back to her fire.

"Ghent," Grietje told her.

"Oh, Ghent! I have many friends in that city. A wonderful place, that it is. Is anything interesting happening there?"

Silence fell. Grietje didn't feel like recounting the events of the day, but she couldn't lie and the woman was waiting. "Two Anabaptists, a woman and a boy, were executed there today," she said.

"Oh…" Maeyken turned sharply and looked into the girl's stricken eyes. "Did you see it?"

"Yes. Well…I heard it. Some of the time I didn't look."

"I see." Maeyken studied Grietje's sensitive face. "No one enjoys seeing something like that. Were they young?"

Grietje covered her face with her hands for an instant. "The boy was about sixteen, it looked to me. The woman had six children. I'm not sure how old she was."

"Hmm. How long?"

Grietje guessed what the woman meant. "Three hours," she whispered.

"Three hours! What cruelty!" Maeyken stopped suddenly. "I mean..." her voice trailed off.

"I know," Grietje reassured her quickly. "The people were stirring. If it hadn't been for all the guards and soldiers about, I think they would have set up a serious protest."

Maeyken held a knife poised over a loaf of bread. "Are you from Ghent?"

"No," Grietje told her, running her fingers along the wall. "I'm on my way home, to Friesland." *I hope she doesn't ask any more questions.*

"Is there a lot of unrest there?" The woman brought the knife down through the soft loaf.

"Not as bad as it is here. A young girl was drowned a little while ago, and there have been a few arrests."

Maeyken looked at Grietje closely. "I've often wondered about those Anabaptists."

Grietje said nothing and averted her eyes. Perhaps Maeyken was laying a clever trap.

"What do you know about them?" Maeyken pried.

Grietje looked back at Maeyken. "They seem to be sincere people. A person would have to be to face that for their faith."

Maeyken's gaze did not leave Grietje's face. "You're one of them, aren't you?"

Grietje was plainly surprised. "Yes, I am."

Maeyken laughed. "Don't worry. I'm harmless. I could tell because you got nervous when I began talking about them."

They sat down to a simple supper in silence. "How could anyone suffer like that just for an idea?" Maeyken asked, almost to herself.

"It's not just an idea, it's the Word of God," Grietje replied gently. "And His grace is sufficient."

• • • • •

Day was fading into the rosy hues of dusk when Grietje reached Dokkum in the evening of January 27, 1544. She devoured the familiar landscapes with her eyes, rejoicing in the sights and sounds and scents of home. Dokkum's ancient walls were sleek and shimmering with patches of ice, wintertime silence bathed the countryside, and the sun drenched the bare trees and tiny houses with warm, vibrant color.

Nevertheless, Grietje slipped inside Dokkum's gates with caution. Long months had passed since her escape and disappearance, but the danger of being recognized and reported still lurked in the alleys and bushes of her native town.

Grietje stopped suddenly in a quiet little corner and looked around her. How wonderful to be back in her own town again! She felt the pocket of her dress; yes, it was there—the letter, Jan's letter, her traitor's letter. How could she give it to him?

Pushing the dismal thoughts aside, the girl smiled to herself as she thought of her family and started on again. How shocked they would be! She quickened her pace, turned down one street and up another, following the curving way unhesitatingly. Her family—she was almost home.

And then they were all around her; her mother was crying and her sisters were laughing and her brothers were staring, wide-eyed.

Supper was forgotten. They wanted to know all about where she had been in the past months; they wanted to hear about Dorcas and Margriete and Levina and David, about every day of her dangerous journey, of every peril and joy and fear. So she told them everything—of her journey to Utrecht, of her long stay there, of the tightening persecution that forced her to start on the fruitless and tearful escape to Ghent. More than an hour and a half passed before the reunited family sat down at the table.

Just before bedtime, Grietje's mother pulled her aside. "But Daughter, what about the letter?"

Chapter 24

The Letter at Last

Is Jan van Aernem still here in Dokkum, Mother?"

Grietje's mother shook her head. "He disappeared more than six months ago. No one knows where he went. I think he was feeling very guilty about Margriete's death. Who wouldn't? Such a sweet, gentle girl—I know you miss her, Grietje."

Grietje stared unseeingly at the door. "I do...and it still hurts so badly. We were very close. I even joined the Doops-gezinde a few weeks before she did, you know, but it always seemed like she was so much more godly than I am."

"But her martyrdom wasn't in vain. One of the girls here who was before violently opposed to us was so touched by

Margriete's courage that she decided to be baptized. Several other people more or less stopped acting hostile."

Light crept into Grietje's eyes. "That's wonderful. Margriete…" her voice died away. "…Margriete would rejoice if she knew."

The mother touched her daughter's shoulder. "I know. You have a lot of catching up to do, Grietje. Things have happened while you were gone."

"But, Mother," a cloud had darkened Grietje's countenance, "what shall I do with this letter? Do you think he would accept it?"

"He might, if you knew where he is."

The girl sighed and gestured helplessly. "Yes, if I only knew where he is…"

• • • •

Many miles away, a young soldier spat on the ground disgustedly. "What's wrong, Jan?" a rough man was prodding him. "Something bothering you this evening?"

Jan's frown deepened. "Don't worry about it," he growled.

Raucous laughter bounced off the rough walls and spread around the circle of young men. "'Don't worry about it,' he says! Come on, Jan-boy, tell me. I'm your friend."

Jan had no intentions of doing so. The truth was, he wanted to go home. Becoming a mercenary in the army of 'Holy Roman Emperor Charles V of Spain' brought no lasting satisfaction. The 'glory' of battle was such a lie. He had longed to become a knight. Surely, that would bring him prestige and respect at last. Instead, his superiors sent him to the front with very little training and expected him to be little more than a servant to these hardened, rough soldiers.

He wanted out! And he was laying devious plans of putting his wishes into action. Somehow, he would return to Dokkum. He was tired of a soldier's life.

War with France had again become a reality. Francis I had been persuaded to sign a peace treaty several years earlier. But now, he had allied himself with the Ottoman Turkish Empire and was ready to do battle once again. Jan knew that desertion was not a small thing. Torture and slow execution was the usual punishment for anyone who may be inclined to leave his post.

Fifteen days passed. Jan became more and more irritable and short-tempered. Finally one night a winter storm darkened the evening sky. Jan's eyes grew brighter and alert in suspense. Perhaps tonight would work. Perhaps tonight he would leave this wretched lifestyle and search for a new beginning.

He lay in the dark for several hours, wide-awake, listening to his comrades' quiet snores. After what seemed like eons of endless and impatient waiting, the young man arose noiselessly and slipped outside into the inky night. He stepped quietly past the dozing guards and headed north, then resolutely made his way toward Dokkum.

Travel was tedious and slow. He was lost almost half the time. He was afraid to show his face to anyone until he was many miles away from the military. The rewards offered for turning in deserters was a great temptation for the poor peasants in the surrounding countryside.

It was three months before he entered the rusty gates of Dokkum. He scowled; the familiar roads and alleys brought back a host of troublesome memories—memories he simply *had* to forget. Jan slouched down the streets of Dokkum and willed his mind to more pleasant things.

. . . . .

Grietje looked up suddenly from her tiresome sewing and glanced out the window. She eyed the young figure moving down the street and gasped. Her needlework fell unheeded to her lap.

"What is it, Daughter?" her mother asked, glancing up in mild alarm.

"Mother! It—it is him, I'm sure of it! It's Jan!"

Both women rose and hastened to the creaky door. "I believe you're right, Grietje. But don't be afraid. I really don't think he'll betray anyone again. Poor boy. He certainly doesn't look very happy."

February stormed in, then March, then April calmed the earth with its gentle breezes. Early flowers dared to show their faces and the fields and trees began to turn green once again. Ice melted in the wake of the budding warmth, and the people rejoiced in the coming of spring.

Many a night Grietje lay awake for several hours wondering and remembering and thinking. *O Lord, what should I do? He seems so hateful. How can I give him the letter? Will he believe it? What will he do with it?*

Finally one breezy spring morning, she rose from her knees by the bed and retrieved the letter. *I have to give it to him. I can't keep it forever. Lord, help me!*

She started toward his foster family's house, but Jan was not there. Grietje turned back. She had no intentions of traipsing around Dokkum in search of her and Margriete's traitor. She sighed. It was hard to keep from harboring evil feelings toward someone who had been Margriete's indirect murderer and very nearly her own.

Footsteps sounded on the street behind her. Grietje ignored them. She had to return home quickly before the wrong person recognized her. Almost she berated herself for starting this fruitless errand.

The crunching sound was nearer now, approaching quickly. Soon whoever it was would overtake her. Grietje quickened her pace; the footsteps behind did too. Something tightened in Grietje's throat and her heart jumped. Was she being followed? She allowed herself a quick, furtive glance over her shoulder, then tripped and almost fell. It was Jan! Would he report her? She slowed again, but this time Jan's pace did not slacken. He passed her.

Grietje forced herself to open her mouth. It was now or never. Her tongue felt like sandpaper.

"Jan," she said softly.

He turned sharply. Grietje studied his face fearfully. Was he still bitter? Would he betray her? Would he turn away? She pulled the precious letter from her pocket. What a story that letter held! "Here is a letter for you."

He shambled toward her. She fought the urge to flee as he approached. Grietje handed him the letter. What if he simply destroyed it? Tears rose in her eyes. "Please believe me. This is not a trick," she said simply, and turned silently away.

Jan looked at it and fingered the seal. He studied the brittle paper, yellowed by the years. Almost disinterestedly he turned it over and glanced at the faint writing. 'To My Only Son,' he read quietly, and jerked erect, thoroughly startled.

He turned and glanced at Grietje, but she was walking away. Could this letter truly be from his own mother? The boy hurried out of the busy town, dropped down beneath a tree, broke the seal, and began to read.

Chapter 25

The Promise of Paradise

Dusk was falling over Dokkum when Grietje left the house. She was going to her first Doopsgezinde meeting in Friesland for almost a year. The path was familiar in the full spring moon, and she hurried toward the shadowy clearing in the woods; she could already hear muffled voices praising their God in song.

How many things had happened since she had met with the believers here! Tears and trials and joys and sorrows... flights and homes and delightful reunions... Impulsively

Grietje lifted her face to the illuminated sky. "Thank you, Lord, for bringing me safely home."

She hurried to the edge of the circle and sat down on the dusty ground beside a tree. The faces were veiled by the forest's gloom, but she recognized one or two. Grietje drank in the hushed sermon and joined wholeheartedly in her people's hymns. Just as the meeting came to an end, the man who had delivered the sermon stood up once more. "We have a young man here tonight," he announced softly, "that has asked to be baptized on confession of his faith."

People who had turned to leave seated themselves once more, and the whole congregation straightened expectantly.

A young man, about eighteen, stood nervously. Grietje strained her eyes through the dim light, but could not recognize him. He looked vaguely familiar. "Who is it?" she whispered to the woman closest to her.

Gasps of surprise and muffled exclamations rippled around the huddled group. "It's Jan!" "Yes, it is!" "Jan van Aernem, the boy who—"

There was no need for explanation. Everyone knew.

Grietje hardly heard Jan's candid testimony. She was dazed by the sudden turn of events. What if he was just playing a trick, to try to trap people into revealing information? It had happened before in other towns. But wait, what was he saying?

"I've done dreadful things, and I'm asking you all to do a very hard thing. Please forgive me. I know I don't deserve it; I've been ultimately guilty for the murder of a girl whom many of you knew and loved. I—it has haunted me ever since. I didn't find any satisfaction in it. Only guilt and fear, even though I didn't at all agree then with Margriete's beliefs.

"Some of you know of a letter I was given. It was fifteen

years old, written by my own mother from prison. It told me things I never dreamed of, and it was the last straw for me. I can't ever undo the crimes I've committed, but I believe that God, in His endless mercy, has forgiven me."

Grietje listened in awe, trying to comprehend. Was this the arrogant boy who had scorned and cursed her many times before? It surely seemed as though he was sincere. She twisted sweaty hands in her lap. "O Lord Jesus, help me to fully forgive him, even as You have forgiven me for my sins. Help me to pardon him for what he's done."

The congregation watched in awe as Jan knelt to be baptized. Surely, this was a transformed young man.

When everyone was talking quietly among themselves, Grietje was shocked to see Jan coming in her direction. She tried to slip away, but she was too late.

"Grietje," he said huskily, looking her full in the face, "I want to tell you I'm very sorry for what I've done to you…and Margriete. I know you were close to her." Jan's eyes were filled with tears.

Grietje hesitated, absentmindedly crunching a dry leaf with the toe of her shoe. Scenes of the time spent in prison flashed before her—the endless interrogations…the fear…the trial… the sentencing…Margriete beside the canal in the last moments of her life…her own flight south…separation…grief…

It was all his fault, after all.

Her fingers turned cold; the silence was oppressive. She forced herself to raise her gaze to Jan's face. "I forgive you," she whispered. And then she felt the enabling power and grace of God fill her soul. As if the words were not her own, she heard herself say softly, "I am very happy for you, Jan… God bless you."

• • • • •

Grietje stole out at dawn the next day and walked slowly toward the city walls. She needed time alone, to think and ponder and pray.

The spring sun was just beginning to rise, a glowing orb peeping above the horizon, touching the buds and flowers with flaming rose and gold. The new grass was tender and fresh, sparkling with morning dew.

Time passed rapidly as she walked toward Leeuwarden. She was deep in thought and the spring air cooled her face. Silently Grietje moved toward the place where Margriete had been martyred and dropped down into the grass. For a long time she gazed into the murky waters, and tears rose in her eyes.

"But," she whispered finally, "Margriete's death brought two souls into the Kingdom, and inspired dozens of others. Even though we are persecuted, He does not forsake us.

"And no matter what we suffer here, there is pure joy in His presence. Someday Margriete and I will see one another again in heaven with the risen Lord. Surely, such a hope is worth the price."